DANGEROUS FORTUNES

Julia takes my fingers and passes my stubby brown nails back and forth along her lips. Eyes running fierce tears, Julia looks into my eyes, and I see the hard sadness of love and try to hold on to it for when she will be gone.

Julia lets out a sigh. "At first it was just that Daddy wanted to get Alden away from the war. Mama would not leave. But she was in shock last Saturday night. You know, she's never wrong reading hands. She says it's like looking through time's window."

"What did she see in their hands?" I ask.

"Nothing," says Julia. "That's just it. Blank skin. The life lines on the first seven hands started strong, but then each one stopped a short way after it began. . . . *Like a map with roads to nowhere*, says Mama. They are all going to die within the next months, India. All."

ALSO AVAILABLE
FROM ROSEMARY WELLS

Mary on Horseback
Leave Well Enough Alone
Through the Hidden Door
When No One Was Looking

Red Moon
at
Sharpsburg

RED MOON

AT

SHARPSBURG

A NOVEL BY

ROSEMARY WELLS

speak

An Imprint of Penguin Group (USA) Inc.

SPEAK
Published by the Penguin Group
Penguin Group (USA) Inc., 345 Hudson Street, New York, New York 10014, U.S.A.
Penguin Group (Canada), 90 Eglinton Avenue East, Suite 700, Toronto, Ontario, Canada M4P 2Y3
(a division of Pearson Penguin Canada Inc.)
Penguin Books Ltd, 80 Strand, London WC2R 0RL, England
Penguin Ireland, 25 St Stephen's Green, Dublin 2, Ireland (a division of Penguin Books Ltd)
Penguin Group (Australia), 250 Camberwell Road, Camberwell, Victoria 3124, Australia
(a division of Pearson Australia Group Pty Ltd)
Penguin Books India Pvt Ltd, 11 Community Centre, Panchsheel Park, New Delhi - 110 017, India
Penguin Group (NZ), 67 Apollo Drive, Rosedale, North Shore 0632, New Zealand
(a division of Pearson New Zealand Ltd)
Penguin Books (South Africa) (Pty) Ltd, 24 Sturdee Avenue,
Rosebank, Johannesburg 2196, South Africa

Registered Offices: Penguin Books Ltd, 80 Strand, London WC2R 0RL, England

First published in the United States of America by Viking,
a member of Penguin Group (USA) Inc., 2007
Published by Speak, an imprint of Penguin Group (USA) Inc., 2008

1 3 5 7 9 10 8 6 4 2

LIBRARY OF CONGRESS CATALOGING-IN-PUBLICATION DATA IS AVAILABLE.

Speak ISBN 978-0-14-241205-3

Printed in the United States of America

For Regina Hayes

Red Moon
at
Sharpsburg

THREE PROMISES

It was my father who found Calvin Trimble's body lying against a stone wall on the Spreckle sisters' land. Pa knew just who it was crumpled up in the hawkweed, still breathing, and somewhere between heaven and earth.

Pa supposed Calvin had been thrown from his horse. He humped the body up across his big shoulders and carried it home to Longmarsh Hall. Tramping through the maze of Trimble fruit orchards, which seem to fill the whole Shenandoah Valley, he had no idea what to expect.

Geneva Trimble was at the front door of Longmarsh Hall. "My God," she said. "His horse came back hours ago! Where did you find him?"

"From down beyond the Spreckles' property," Pa answered. Pa heaved Calvin up the grand staircase. With a hand holding him gingerly under the neck, he lay Calvin in his bed like a sleeping baby. Micah Cooley, the Trimbles' head house servant, was dispatched at a run to fetch Doctor Hooks.

In the bedroom, Pa could hear the midges hum louder than Calvin's little bird breaths. Emory, the oldest of three Trimble sons, was then seven and sickly with asthma. Eyes never leaving his father, Emory crawled into his mother's spacious lap. Geneva Trimble, then and now, is as big as a boulder.

"Em-ry, you get out of here or you'll start up your asthma," ordered Geneva. Emory paid her no mind but studied his father's moon-white face.

"I have seen you in church, Sundays," whispered Geneva to Pa, although there was no need to whisper.

"I am Cyrus Moody," said Pa, remembering to take off his hat. "I'm the harness maker lives in Berryville. I have made three sets of driving tack for Mr. Calvin. Your husband's a good customer, ma'am."

"You carried him two miles," Geneva said to my pa.

"Weren't heavy, ma'am," said Pa. Pa took up Calvin's wrist. "He's got a pulse," Pa said with a little flat hope in his voice. Geneva smoothed the wrinkles out of the bed's counterpane. Waiting for the doctor, Pa took note of her unblinking eyes. It seemed to him she was attempting to will the life back into Calvin with those eyes.

"He is trying to come back," Pa said to Geneva.

"Do you think he can hear us?"

Pa answered, "I think he can. He has three growing boys, ma'am. They need their father. My wife is expecting our firstborn, maybe next week. How would that child go forth in the world without a father?"

Doctor Junius Hooks peered into a lens, through Calvin's irises to the back wall of the eyes. When he had looked at both eyes, he snapped his pocket lens shut and pronounced the brain to be swollen inside the head. There was nothing a doctor could do with a probable fractured skull.

Doctor Hooks told Geneva that her husband was in his last hour of life. He walked young Emory out of the room, told him to stop biting his fingernails and to prepare his brothers, Tom and Rupert, for their father's passing.

"You are going to bring on Emory's asthma, Junius," said Geneva.

"He must learn to control the asthma," said Doctor Hooks.

Pa's leather-hard hand picked up Geneva Trimble's fingers as if they were made of eggshell. At the head of Calvin's bed stood Micah Cooley and his wife, Ester. "One to each side, standing like the Sphinxes at the Temple of Nineveh," Geneva would say from that day forward.

To this day also, Geneva Trimble insists that a circle of fire suddenly rose over Calvin's bed when Ester Cooley began to pray aloud. The Lord's voice spoke, not in an ancient biblical language, but in the King's English any person could understand. It was Ester's prayers that stopped Calvin just short of the gates of heaven and turned him earthward. It was Ester's prayers that got Calvin sitting up and asking for his favorite Floating Island pudding, with nothing worse wrong than a stiff neck.

In gratitude to my pa, Geneva Trimble made her first promise of the day to him. "Calvin and I will protect your household and children for all the days we have left on the earth. You must never again call me ma'am or Mrs. Trimble."

In gratitude to Ester, a second Trimble promise was made. Ester and Micah Cooley were granted their freedom. So that they would never be in want, they were also granted their own orchard land.

Calvin Trimble asked that his will be brought to him on the might-could chance he fell back in a coma. The will was taken from its safe, which lay in a hidden room behind the library. Geneva led my pa downstairs, and he watched her disappear into a revolving panel in a bookcase. Pa examined the hidden spring and the carpentry and admired it.

Calvin Trimble deeded over to Ester and Micah Cooley a good mule, a cart, and ten acres of their best Belle of Georgia peach trees. Tears filled Micah and Ester Cooley's eyes, as the promise was solemnly made and the will changed to include the Cooleys. My pa witnessed the new will with his signature, and so it was a legal document.

The third promise of the day was made not by Geneva Trimble, but by the Spreckle sisters. Earlier that day they had watched from their vegetable garden as Pa hauled Calvin off their property. At a decent distance they had followed Pa up to Longmarsh Hall, bearing arnica root.

Being very polite, the sisters did not want to interfere with the goings-on. Actually, no one even knew they were in the house. During the promising and the solemn changing of Calvin's will, the Spreckle sisters perched unseen, like twin hedgehogs, in the library wing chairs. They only wished to offer their arnica root to Calvin as helpful neighbors.

Naturally, the sisters overheard every word about freedom, transference of property, and white servants' wages to Ester and Micah Cooley. These things were just not done in the state of Virginia in the year 1848.

They also watched Geneva Trimble press a hidden lever behind the *World Atlas* and disappear into a revolving bookcase with her husband's will.

Only when she came out again did Geneva notice the sisters, little beady eyes all merry, in their wing chairs with their arnica root in a basket.

Geneva made the Spreckles swear an oath that they would not tell about anything they had seen or heard that day.

"Of course we will promise," said Eloise Spreckle, "on the Bible itself!"

"It is nobody's business outside this family!" agreed

Grace. So the sisters' was the third solemn promise of the day.

I was born a week later, according to my pa, exactly at the appearance of the evening star. Geneva Trimble attended my birth. As was the custom she sat at the head of the bed and kneaded Mama's hands with orange-seed oil, allowing all the work of yanking-out to be done by the Granny woman. I was scrawny, green eyed like my pa, with a full shock of coal-black hair like my mama. Mama wanted to call me Edna, but Geneva would have no Ednas. She rolled her eyes heavenward and said, "This is a Trimble godchild!" She insisted, "Edna's a pokey name! Look at those big green Indian eyes!"

Pa suggested, "We will call her India."

India Moody I became.

Micah and Ester Cooley became free Virginians, who profited from their own ten acres of orchard land. Geneva Trimble's two promises at Calvin's bedside were kept. As for the Spreckle sisters' promise, it, too, was kept faithfully, until it was dusted with a little time.

All else that followed during the war came of those three promises, two kept and one broken, made the week before I was born.

Time's Window

When you first see me, it is July 30, 1861. I, India Moody, am twelve years old. I am still green of eye, crow-black of hair, and I am still a skinny-minnie. I am looking out the window of our little three-room house on Buckmarsh Street in Berryville, Virginia. Berryville is not nearly as grand as our west neighbor, Winchester, not nearly as busy as our north neighbor, Harpers Ferry, but it is a fine town nonetheless and smack in the middle of the Shenandoah Valley, which many people compare to heaven itself. We have the general store, the farrier and livery stable, the Clarke County Courthouse, our school, and lots of people's houses, brick and wood, fancy and plain, and three churches. Everyone I have ever known my twelve years on the earth lives hereabouts in the valley. Our farmers are so prosperous, people say, the soil of our pastures so rich, that you can throw a handful of seeds in the air and have corn on the cob the next day.

You'll see my face staring out our window impatiently. I am waiting for my best friend, Julia Pardoe. Quite soon her father will drive up in their new black carriage with the gold paint trim, pulled by a favorite pair of chestnut geldings. I am perched on our pine table in a borrowed silk dress, swinging my feet. I have scuffed the blacking my mama has carefully applied to her good shoes, which I have also borrowed.

We are going to a gala celebration at Longmarsh Hall, home of my Trimble godparents. Before too long the Pardoes' carriage stops before our house and I get in. The horses snort and stamp. Their harness, made by my pa, squeaks and jingles pleasantly. It is a hot night. The horses are already lathered and glad for a small rest. My pa steps out into the street with a bucket of water for them. He slicks some sweat foam off the near horse's withers and says hello to Julia's family.

"Come along with us, the whole county's invited," says Mr. Pardoe.

"Got to keep an eye on the old man and the little sprout," says Pa, sloshing the water pail under the other horse's muzzle. Pa and Mama have to stay home with my little brother, Eddie, and old Grandpa, since he is likely to wander off the moment he is alone.

I sit back between Julia and her brother Alden and watch as Berryville jounces past. The party at the Trimbles' will celebrate the war's first great Southern victory, Manassas, where the Yankees threw away their guns, turned tail like the cowards they are, and handed the field to us. It is with clear rousing joy that most people greet the news of our victory, but Julia's parents are Quakers. They hate war and all its glowing talk. They do not own slaves. They are only going to this party because Mr. Pardoe is the most important lawyer in town and Calvin Trimble his most important client. No one wants to hurt the Trimbles' feelings, so the Pardoes have agreed to go.

"Lots and lots of newly minted junior officers tonight," Julia whispers to me, "just waiting to kiss the girls goodbye!" We have been talking about this for days, Julia and me. We do like seeing the boys in uniform. We can't take our eyes off them when they walk down the street, trousers pressed and gold gleaming from their cuffs and stripes.

Parthenia Pardoe, Julia's mother, overhears her and arches her eyebrow. "Let us hope and let us pray," she says, "that this celebration of war will be the last of its kind. We want no more dancing on the graves of any innocent young men. Blue or gray, thank you."

"Wishful thinking, my dear," replies Mr. Pardoe. He clucks his horses on with relish over the plain dirt road to Longmarsh. "The war will be long and brutal."

"And I will be left out of it entirely," says Alden. He stares angrily out at a horse pasture, home to a couple of dozen gleaming Thoroughbreds who graze happily in the lingering July evening. "I can hardly look Tom and Rupert

Trimble in the eye I am so embarrassed," he adds, fairly spitting the words. "They joined up. Why can't I?"

Suddenly Alden pulls a Virginia Grays kepi cap out from his pocket and puts it on. His father pulls the horses to a halt, stopping the carriage.

"Alden," says Mr. Pardoe in his best courtroom voice, "take the cap off."

"No, Father, I am sorry but I will not," says Alden.

"Well, then you may leave us and walk the rest of the way."

"Just wait," says Alden. "I will join up! I look eighteen. Who's to know I'm sixteen?"

"Alden, you look all of twelve to me," says Julia.

He ignores her but goes a little bit red above the collar.

"You are a Quaker," his father reminds him. "And a Quaker does not bear arms or raise his hand to smite another man. You will be shunned if you talk of fighting in the war."

"All the boys are joining up," whines Alden. "All the boys call me a slacker. Next year it will be the first thing I will do. Shunning be hanged!"

Because I am in the carriage and Julia's father hates raised voices, he only frowns his son out of his seat. Alden has a point. If a boy isn't *in the war* he might as well sing high soprano in the church choir. A way will be found, I tell myself, for Alden's military ambitions to be avoided.

I tell the Pardoe carriage, "My pa says the fighting will

be over by October anyway. Pa says Abe Lincoln's army has only signed on for a ninety-day stint. The Union soldiers just won't stay in the South and fight. They'll throw down their guns and go home to take in their own harvests."

"It's true! It *will* be over in three months' time!" Alden chimes in from the roadside. "It will be *all* over! All my friends will have served and I'll be called a coward forever after!"

"Have a nice walk, dear," says his mother pleasantly.

Julia's father smiles seriously and releases the horses to a smart trot.

In his sensible voice, he explains, "No doubt your father knows what he is talking about, my dear India. Nonetheless it will be a deadly long war because it was started by stubborn men, mule-stubborn men, here in the South. They want to have the War of the Roses all over again. They're licking their lips over the prospect of great heroes and great battles. They'll never give in, and their war's likely to kill half our young men."

Mr. Pardoe studies his wife's face. Parthenia hates talk of war. She leans out, looking to see where Alden is. Mr. Pardoe watches her keenly. "You don't pick a fight with a bully twice your size," he continues. "The North will draft as many young men as they need into a war machine and they will slaughter us. I am inclined to leave the valley until it's over and somebody picks up the pieces."

Julia has told me her father has received a letter from his sister in Ohio. The sister claims to have it from the highest sources that President Lincoln will deal with the South as King Herod massacred the Jews of Bethlehem.

"Girls!" says Parthenia Pardoe as Longmarsh Hall comes into distant view. "Geneva Trimble's invitation says that shortly after everyone arrives, the band will stop playing and there will be a moment of silent prayer for the men who have died. We will remember Mr. Reed and pray to rest his soul in comfort. He is our first death."

School had ended in Berryville very suddenly in late April. There were seven boys and thirteen girls in our single-room class. The door was locked one Monday morning, and a notice nailed to it. We gathered around and read the notice every which way.

School is closed until after the war is won!
I will see you in three months.
Read your Scriptures and practice your tables.
John R. Reed, Captain, 11th Virginia Cavalry

Mr. Reed was the only teacher in Berryville. He had changed his name to Captain Reed. The members of our class skipped home after reading the sign. Most of them hated the multiplication tables, which we had to recite each morning after prayer, but I was not so sure. I was good at the multiplication tables. I practiced them when I polished

Pa's harness brasses and scrubbed the dishes. I knew the tables by heart after the first week because I could see the logic to them in the eye of my mind. Mr. Reed lent me books without either of us telling anyone else. Then I'd write a five-paragraph essay on the story. The latest was a brand-new novel, *David Copperfield*. Mr. Reed's closing the school was a severe disappointment to me.

"Oh, joy! We get a nice early summer holiday!" piped up Julia, who would not memorize beyond three times four. Julia hated school. Me, Julia, and all the other members of our class were sucked back into home lives. Our following existence became an endless row of Saturdays. Then Mr. Reed was shot in the head, July 21, a Sunday morning, at the battle of Manassas.

The horses are halted once more and their reins taken by footmen. We alight from our carriage and are received in the garden by the two younger Trimble sons, Tommy and Rupert. Both are already in uniform. They are such beautiful boys, their gray tunics and white gloves spotless. Mr. Pardoe smiles at them indulgently. He has known them all their lives, but you can see in his eyes the military uniforms make Julia's father anxious.

I walk between Parthenia and Julia into the entrance of Longmarsh Hall. The double doors are wide open to the world. The doorway is framed in an arbor of flowering trumpet vines, orange blossoms trailing in carefully pruned bowers.

There is a strict pattern to how people live according to their calling in life. The Trimbles are landowners of an old Virginia family. Longmarsh Hall was built on a rise by Lucas Trimble, lieutenant governor of Virginia, many years ago. There are two large parlors, front and back, a music room, a dining hall that seats two dozen guests, seven bedrooms, and a clerestory that sits atop the roof.

The Pardoes are not nearly as rich as the Trimbles, but Julia's house is much finer than mine. It is brick, with four bedrooms, a servants' hall, and land on the other edge of town. Always at the Pardoes' dinner table I am reminded of my place in life's scale as a tradesman's daughter. The Pardoes have real silver to eat with. It sits gleaming and heavy in the hand. The forks do not need their tines straightened after each meal as my mama's tin forks do.

As we pass through the front door, Julia's mother, Parthenia, leans over and reminds us. "Remember," she says, "not a word to anyone about you-know-what. I hate doing it in public places."

She is referring to palm reading. At one time Parthenia explained her special talent to me. "The life line is a crease across the palm of the left hand. Even babies have them. A good life line goes strongly from thumb to wrist. There is a head line, a love line, and so forth across the whole span of the hand. Those little ruckles along the line mean children, illness, money. All major events in a person's life can be sorted out this way beforehand. If you know how, a palm is as easy to read as a signpost."

Julia and I get chased up to the second floor, where we lean over the balcony railing of the grand staircase to view events. From our high perch we can witness everything worth knowing about. Holding our fingers just so, we sip from flutes of ginger beer, pretending it is champagne punch.

A pack of pretty girls, just a few years older than me and Julia, flirt outrageously downstairs. They cannot get enough of the uniforms on the boys. The boys, trying to look entirely ho-hum, strut up and down in smart trousers with stripes up the side. They will, soon enough, be in what will be called the Army of Northern Virginia but isn't called much of anything yet. I squirm to run my fingers along the boys' wool sleeves, along the wide gold bands, to feel it prickle and see if the braid is real gold.

Beside me is Julia, whose smooth hair falls onto her shoulders. For a moment I let my imagination play on Julia's face. One fine day shiploads of boys will admire her comely shape and try to run their fingers through her silky gold hair. My hair is unruly and my body hopelessly unwomanly.

Every so often a sketch artist comes to the Pardoes' house. Using a sheet and lamp, he creates a shadow profile and traces the exact silhouette of Alden's and Julia's faces in black against white. Julia's mother predicts the beautiful profile Julia will have when she grows up. A woman's patrician breeding is revealed in the bone structure of her face.

Julia is not biggity. She doesn't care about bone structure. She doesn't care that her pa is a top-rail lawyer and mine only a harness maker. She and I are close as sisters born under the same roof. Our twelve summers together have been spent sprinting around in the two thousand acres of Trimble orchards, which circle out into the Shenandoah Valley of Virginia, almost to the Winchester road.

In the summer the trees are heavy with each different season of fruit. First come cherries, then figs and peaches, then apples, grapes, and pears. All are wrapped in tissue, boxed, and sent to Richmond by railroad where the greengrocer wholesalers pay top dollar.

Julia and I devoured Elephant Heart plums carelessly, throwing the pits as far as we could throw, leaping over windfallen cherries, red mouthed as if we were fillies in heaven.

But now, all of that comes to a sudden end, as the pears take over from the cherries in the summer of 1861.

The Spreckle sisters advise some of the guests that

Julia's mother is a gifted palm reader. From our perch on the upstairs banister of Longmarsh Hall, Julia and I watch events below. Down in the stairwell, Parthenia backs into view, urged along by a set of tee-heeing girls. Her secret is out. Julia's mother keeps insisting, "No! I won't do it. I am not a fortune-teller. My gift is not meant as a parlor game. Go ahead and dance with your sweethearts, my dears! The orchestra is playing for you."

"The Spreckles have told!" whispers Julia. "Mother will give them a piece of her mind when she gets a chance. She hates to be treated like a gypsy fortune-teller."

I gaze dreamily down at the top of Parthenia's head. Chestnut braids wing off both sides of a center part. She has pinned them in a perfect circle with silver combs. I can hear the rustle of her silk dress and the satisfactory clicking of the pearls in her necklace.

Parthenia Pardoe surrenders. She begins to look at the offered palms, turned upward under the lamplight. Seven young soldiers and their girls are backed up into the parlor. I count them. More couples pack onto the back of the line. Parthenia examines the boys' palms as thoughtfully as a doctor looking for splinters. She goes through the first seven boys, saying nothing. We know them all, Bayley Buck and his brother, Will, Abe Spengler, Hap Stuckey, the Hammersmith boys. Suddenly, Parthenia's punch cup spills onto the floor.

"Something's wrong," says Julia suddenly, not bothering to whisper.

"She should have eaten something!" voices advise around Parthenia Pardoe's fallen body. "Too little air on a hot night!" "The punch was deceptively strong!"

Geneva Trimble intervenes. She raises Julia's mother to her feet and half walks, half carries Parthenia upstairs to her bedroom.

A servant brings valerian drops in a glass of water. Then Julia's father closes the door, and there is nothing more to be known. Two days pass before I find out what really happened that night at Longmarsh Hall.

Julia wanders down Buckmarsh Street to our house to tell me. She is all lavender and white in a new gingham dress. I am standing outside our front door in a patch of shade. It is an uncommonly hot afternoon.

Inside the house Eddie is cranky with sweat and the bores. Mama wants me to bathe him off. I am about to go over to the pump in the yard when Julia appears on the street. Her frown is set like a funeral face.

She says, "We are leaving Berryville. We have to go to Ohio to live with Papa's cousins. We have to wait out the war in the North."

"No," I say stupidly. "No! No!"

"Yes," says Julia. "Father has entered Alden at Oberlin College, away from all his friends with war fever. He will matriculate in September."

"What is 'Oberlin College'?" I ask. "What is 'matriculate'?"

Out from Julia's pocket comes a well-creased letter. It is another from her father's sister in Ohio. There are words underlined: "We have heard from Mary Lincoln, now in the exact center of everything of the world. She has it straight from President Lincoln himself that a rain of blood will fall upon the South, turning the very map of Virginia red."

I do not understand this talk. All our newspapers are full of the Southern victory.

I read the letter twice. "But we won!" I say to Julia, holding back tears at the injustice. "The South won the war in Manassas last week! We whipped the mickeys off the Yanks. The whole Yankee army turned tail and ran like girls up Bull Run Creek!"

Julia chews a strand of hair and uses my baby name. "Tiddy, Mama says you can come on the train to Ohio with us and live with us! The cousins have a big house on the hill that sleeps twenty. We could ride all the horses in my uncle's stable."

Julia does not wait for me to say no. She does not want to hear that I could never leave Mama with all the chores of running our family, that I have no money for a railway ticket. Julia has no chores at home.

"Just ask your mama and pa if you can come," pleads Julia. "Just ask. It won't hurt to just ask!"

Out of my mouth come no words at all. Of course we

both know at bottom that Julia and I come from two sepa-
rate classes of people, but never have we cared about social
stations. We purposely never cared. Now this ugliness rises
between us. Mama's voice speaks in my head, *The Pardoes
have every choice money can buy: servants, travel, education. We
have few choices. So be content, India, with what the Lord has
given you.*

Julia takes my fingers and passes my stubby brown nails
back and forth along her lips. Eyes running fierce tears,
Julia looks into my eyes, and I see the hard sadness of love
and try to hold on to it for when she will be gone.

Julia lets out a sigh. "At first it was just that Daddy
wanted to get Alden away from the war. Mama would not
leave. But she was in shock last Saturday night. You know,
she's never wrong reading hands. She says it's like looking
through time's window."

"What did she see in their hands?" I ask.

"Nothing," says Julia. "That's just it. Blank skin. The life
lines on the first seven hands started strong, but then each
one stopped a short way after it began. . . . *Like a map with
roads to nowhere,* says Mama. They are all going to die within the next months, India. All."

WAR GAMES

Road dirt, feather soft, covers my bare toes. I wait endlessly for a letter from Julia, going to the Berryville post office each evening, but no letter comes. The last I saw her was through the dusty window of the Winchester train bound for Harpers Ferry and the Baltimore and Ohio Railroad beyond. One minute she was waving to me, the next she vanished like a bird sailing into a white sky. One month later it is as if she had never been born.

Oberlin, Ohio, sounds to be hundreds of miles away. I have no map of where it might be. I wander through the Trimble orchards alone, remembering our favorite songs and hideout spots. There is nothing to do without school and no best friend, so I play war with the town boys, Frawley Turpin, Jimmy Ray Cox, and their friends, me dressed in boy's clothes.

When I come home Mama says, "I ought to wash you down with lye soap, India Moody. You're no better'n a billy goat let into the house."

"Yes, ma'am," I say.

I promise Mama, for the tenth time, not to associate again with the boys.

Pa and I oil up a brand-new harness. I love the smell of the leather and the tung oil that is used to soften and finish it. It settles me to watch Pa's careful hands fly across and around the thick new leather that makes the traces and straps. He hangs them on wooden bars. These racks cover all of one parlor wall. I say parlor, but we have only three rooms, two up and one big one down for kitchen, eating, and sitting.

"India," says Pa. "Your ma and I want you to keep up your book learning and stay away from those town boys."

"But school is closed!"

"While the war is on, you must be tutored. Emory Trimble has agreed to teach you your lessons until the war ends and school is open again. That won't be long."

"Yes, sir," I say. I have always liked Emory Trimble, the oldest son, who is not in the army. Emory is all red hair and busy fingers. Emory is smart as a snake, but too rattle-chested from his asthma to be more than a Sunday soldier.

"I wish India could be with young ladies, too," Ma puts in. "The Lord did not intend young girls to play boys' games with a pack of ruffians. You hear me, India?"

Awl in hand, Pa pierces a perfectly even line of one hundred thread holes along a seven-inch leather strap. He does this in no time at all, as if the leather were a handkerchief. Later, in his shop, he will run a steel needle bearing heavy thread through the holes.

Pa frowns. "Can't you find new young lady friends here in Berryville?" he asks.

I grump. "I hate talking about dresses and church socials. Julia is gone, and the other girls all have best friends. They don't want me."

Mama makes a clicking noise with her tongue. She is setting the sleeves into a new shirt for Pa. "Young lady," she says, voice snipping along with her scissors, "I don't want to hear again about you running around with that pack of white-trash mongrels, Jimmy Ray Cox and Frawley Turpin, and neither does our Lord Jesus."

"Mama, won't you ever sing to us anymore?" I ask. Mama is known for the sweetest singing voice in our church choir. She does the solos with pride each Sunday. At home the easy slapping sound of Pa's leather, accompanied by Mama's singing, has always meant complete happiness to me.

"I'll sing when my work is done and the cows come home," says Mama.

Ma is crabby about something more than me. Eddie chews on his thumb and whimpers. Grandpa Moody, age ninety-one, rocks and sucks the marrow out of an empty lamb chop bone. You wouldn't dare grab the bone away from him.

"Where are you, Grandpa Moody?" I ask him, shouting.

"Visiting in heaven," he rasps. Grandpa Moody's mind turns white half the time. It comes on when Mama's snappish or didn't take time to cut up his food how he likes it.

Something is also eating at Pa. His jittery thigh won't sit still a minute. Ma hates it when Pa's jumpy and won't say why.

On the second Sunday in September a stranger preaches to us in church. His name is Senator John Randolph Tucker and his sermon is all about the war.

He begins with Leviticus. Forefinger in air, he quotes from memory. "Both thy bondmen and thy bondmaids shall be of the heathen that are round about you. The children of strangers shall ye buy and of their families they shall be your possessions. They shall be your bondmen forever!"

Tucker then slides into the Yankees trying to change the natural order of the world as ordained by the Bible, Moses, and God himself.

"Slippery-palmed money changers," Tucker calls the Yankees, "sitting in their Northern temples counting the gold they had stolen from honest Virginia farmers."

I am church-sleepy in the third pew on the right. You can bet that I and every other good Presbyterian could easily picture those palms slippery with hair oil counting stacks of gold coins the height of a good-size tree.

Tucker's words are as pretty as a peddler's pearls. Tears

fill eyes in church that morning. Farmers bite their lips and rub the calluses of their hands.

From the pastures drift the bleats of young lambs and ewes. I close my eyes.

Bang! goes the edge of Tucker's hand on the pulpit, and I wake with a start. "The South will rise like Israel in the days of David! The bloodsucker Abe Lincoln will die by our sword! Now who will sign up to do the Lord's work today?" Tucker sews it all up.

A dozen men shuffle up and volunteer for the Clarke County Rifles. They sign up with a sergeant that Senator Tucker's got squirreled away in his carriage. Many of them make the sign of the X and Tucker fills out their names in plain script because they cannot write. My pa does not join the volunteers, but I see his eyes look far-offish.

We are standing on the steps of the church, waiting to shake the hand of John Randolph Tucker. Behind us the sky is sweet blue and the birds sing all around. Mama straightens the waist of her dress and observes, "I bet Mammy Tucker just loved that dimple in her darlin's chin."

"Polly, you've got a catty woman's tongue today," says Pa. He cleans something out of the heel of his boot. Pa is squinty eyed looking into the sun, no smile from him all the way home. He walks fast in front of Mama and Eddie and me.

Mama is not shy about saying what she thinks. "Tucker's

nothing but a recruiting agent. When the government starts preaching war from the pulpit, the poor and simple who sit in the pews will follow it like God's word. But it is a clever politician's word, not God's word."

That day much talking gets done between Mama and Pa alone and away from me. I pretend to be taking care of Eddie but I get him to start piling his blocks and quick run to the door to listen to what they say.

Pa wants to move our family to Mama's brother Peter's home in Kettletown, in western Virginia. Kettletown is out of the way of the war. Brother Peter has sent word that we are expected until the war is done. Aunt Divine has begun a sewing shop and needs every extra hand she can get. Mama won't hear of it. I hold my breath and pray that this will not happen. Uncle Peter and Aunt Divine believe the color red to be sinful and never let you forget that they are in charge of every little thing.

Sunday evening there is a stony air between Mama and Pa. I sit next to Pa while he takes apart an old saddle he is set to repair. I ask him, "I don't understand why there has to be a war. Is Lincoln really a bloodsucking Judas, Pa? Is he going to free all slaves and send 'em back to Africa?"

"The war isn't over the Southern slaves, Pussy Willow," Pa says. "Half Lincoln's army'd walk away home if he tried to free the slaves."

"Then why are the Yanks down here fighting us, Pa?"

"It's simple," Pa says. "The Yanks are trying to take over

our land. They're down here like a plague of locusts killing Virginia farmers, stealing Virginia cattle."

"But why, all of a sudden?" I ask.

"They want what we have and they want to change our Southern way of life."

I still do not understand why there is a war. I ask, "Pa, if the Yanks are *not* trying to free the slaves and we're *not* fighting to keep slavery, then why'd the little South pick such a big fight with the North? Why, Pa?"

"They started it. We didn't," Pa answers with a rumple in his voice.

I'm not allowed to argue anymore.

The subject of the war does not come up again. It is a great mystery how and when grown-up people decide things. Much goes on in a world just behind my back that I am not allowed to see or hear. The grown-ups tell me when all is decided, and I have nothing to say about it.

The following Sunday night I am in bed and looking at the stars out my window. On my pillow is my doll, Abby. Pa made her for me when I was five, with horsetail hair and blue bead eyes that were bought from a peddler and said to be from Persia.

Pa pokes his head in at my door. "I am away tomorrow," he announces gruffly. He has brought his new sergeant's tunic in for me to see. "Look at the gold braid on the sleeves," he says, sitting on my bed and offering it to me. "Feel how nice that is!"

But I don't want to touch it. I bury my face in his lap. "Why?" I ask.

He goes on. "Well, Tiddy, I saw the wounded from some skirmish up at Beller's Mill. There's fresh wounded men and still wounded from Manassas all over the pews of the church. Nowhere to put 'em up. People are taking the wounded into their homes, but there isn't a way on God's earth to transport the Carolina boys with no legs and half their faces gone back down to home again. Hundreds more of 'em in Winchester. If I do not serve and help our neighbors I will hang my head in shame."

I let a little time pass. Pa sits on my bed and takes my hands in his. "I'm looking for my star," I say. "The one that came out when I was born?"

"Venus," says Pa. "Evening star."

"Where is Cassiopeia, Pa?"

"Over there."

"Can we name all the constellations?"

"Yes, we can."

"Will they be the same stars where you are going, Pa?"

"Yes, I believe so."

"How far away from home have you been in your life, Pa?"

"Maybe down to Luray. Up to Harpers Ferry. Maybe even fifty miles."

"That's a long way. Longer than I've ever been. I've been five miles, I guess."

"I may be sent to Richmond. The Yanks want to attack Richmond and take the Confederate Capitol down." Pa rubs his chin.

"Richmond is far away as the moon."

Pa closes my eyes for me with his fingertips. "Are you going to mind your mama and help her?"

"Pa, do I ever *not* help her?"

He says, "Eddie has a nasty boil. It can go festerous in a day. Take him up to Trimbles. Ask Emory Trimble to look at it."

I ask timidly, "Are they getting better, Pa? The wounded soldiers . . . are they going to live?"

Pa answers, "Some. Lots of them have septic fevers and gangrene. Junius Hooks has been tending them without sleep for two days." Pa covers his eyes and rubs them, as if to blot out a thought. "I had to do something awful," he says. "I had to bring Isaac Hockney's body to his mama and papa today. Killed at Beller's Mill. Lucy Hockney was in the front yard. She was very brave."

A chill goes over me. Isaac Hockney was the first one in Parthenia Pardoe's line.

"Will you kill Yanks, in the army, Pa? Will you shoot them?"

He takes a long time to think this question over. "I think a man can't tell that until the time comes," he says softly, "and then he knows whether he can shoot another man or not. I've asked to be billeted with the horses and supply wagons."

"Pa?"

"Yes, my angel?" asks Pa.

I tell him, "Mr. Reed won't come back. He is dead."

"That is why I have to go," says Pa. "Because some cock-eyed strangers came down here and killed your school-teacher."

"Don't stay long, Pa!"

"Just ninety days, that's all it will take," Pa says.

I place ninety kisses into my cupped hand and then into the pocket of his tunic and I close the button on the pocket so that the kisses cannot spill out. "Take one out each day that you are away," I tell him.

At first light Pa comes in again. "Be good to Mama," he says.

"I am always good to Mama."

"You are your papa's girl," he says. "Don't argue with your mama." His voice is worried. "Don't forget to take Eddie first thing this morning." He holds my face in both hands. In his hair I smell leather and tung oil. Pa and I hold hands and let our eyes swim in the immensity of the dawn through the four-inch panes of my window.

Mama has been up half the night making him a saddle-bag dinner. Pa must join a regiment twenty miles away in Fairfax County. Biscuits and fried chicken and ham go into it. Apples. A bottle of buttermilk wrapped in newspaper to keep it cool, all in the bag. "Don't give it away to the other men. Save it for yourself."

In the street outside our house Mama can't pull enough air into her lungs. He kisses her and tries to make her smile but her face is bitter.

"Oh, Cy, Cy, Cy," Mama cries. She is in a sudden panic. "Please change your mind. Please don't get killed. Please, Cy, say your prayers every night."

Up goes Pa onto our bay mare's back, Maybelle, the one who long ago gave a few hairs of her tail for my doll, Abby. He blows a kiss, and Maybelle's hooves scuff up, sparking gravel as she turns. Then he is not there at all. Just a little dust devil on the road.

I lean my head against the bodice of Mama's dress and watch Eddie's giddy little feet kicking.

Neither Mama nor I want to take our eyes off the spot where Maybelle turned and trotted off.

At breakfast Mama gives Eddie bits of ground-up clabber and ham. Eddie only eats sugar-cured, and this kind is too salty for him.

"India," Mama says, "things will be different. I must head this house now. It means more work for you. Taking Eddie, taking Grandpa off me."

"Yes, ma'am," I answer. Work that never ends is what happens to women. Women try and feed every mouth in the house, and the mouths just spit out half of what comes in.

In the street outside two boys are making boy-only jokes. They are in uniform. I know who they are. They come into Pa's shop all the time. They want to get right *in it* soon in case the war is over before they have a chance to fight.

I go to Pa's storeroom at the back of our house. I breathe in his smell in the neatly oiled leather straps and the shirt and trousers that hang there. In the stillness of the room, the clothes, leather, and I all wait for him to come back.

Later I ask Mama, "Why? Why did he have to go?"

She takes a while to answer. "It's men. There's something in the blood," Mama says. "It's the way things are. Women settle differences with sharp tongues. Men settle things with fists and bullets. They can't ever get enough."

"Not Pa," I plead with her.

"Seems to me," she says, "the whole town's worth of men just dropped their plows and pencils and walked into the army like flowers turning to the sun."

The Garden
of Temptations

Because of Emory's asthma, Calvin Trimble commissioned a room of glass panes to be built onto the dining room at Longmarsh Hall. Glass houses are common, Calvin says, in cold climates, but his is the first in Virginia. People come to stare at it. The glass house was filled with ferns, watered every day. The resulting air condensed like the inside of a cloud. Emory could breathe at night, and he grew stronger. When he was sixteen, he packed up his rucksack like Lewis and Clark and visited the Indians in Tennessee. Emory says they cured his asthma by feeding him small doses of arsenic.

Emory, still shallow chested and now twenty, is closed away in his glass house writing furiously. He wouldn't lift his head if a black widow spider crawled out of his inkwell. Mama and I await him with Eddie and his boil.

"That boy of mine will not come out of his glass temple," says Geneva.

Eddie is squirming in my mama's lap. He won't let anyone touch his foot.

Ester Cooley raps on the pane of Emory's glass house with a coffee spoon to get his attention. Suddenly a shock of red curly hair enters the sitting room. Expertly Emory fingers Eddie's boil. He cleans it with red oak fluid, which makes Eddie scream.

"It's an antiseptic," says Emory.

Antiseptic is a word I have never heard.

Emory disappears and comes back with a handful of black moss. This he places on the boil and ties in place with a handkerchief before Eddie catches his first screaming breath in my mother's arms.

"Keep it in place," Emory says. "Tomorrow it will not hurt him anymore. The next day it should be gone."

"What did you put on it?" asks my mama.

"Bread mold," says Emory, "called penicillium, in a dressing of Irish moss. That's a seaweed. A student of mine sends it dried from Baltimore."

Baltimore is a place I have never imagined being actually real. I have never heard of anyone I know who sent anything or visited there.

Mama purses her lips and does not ask about it further. Instead she says, "We have brought India's study book from school for you to begin her lessons."

I want to ask more about the bread mold and Irish moss and how he knows to use them. Holding a copy of *Mackey's Moral*

Behavior under my arm, I follow Emory out of the room.

I have never been allowed into Emory's glass house before. It is his private laboratory. Ferns of all kinds hang in suspended pots. Sunlight, seen through the many panes and fronds, is dappled yellow-green above us. The shelves are filled with flasks and books and jars. The brick floor is a mass of different plants, holders competing for sun space. Everything is labeled in terrible handwriting.

A stuffed barn owl, soft and fat as a purse, peers at me through his glass eyes.

"His name is Buddha," says Emory.

"What does 'Booda' mean?" I ask.

"Buddha is the name of God in China," says Emory. "Buddha is a fat bald man, unlike Jesus."

"There are other gods?" I ask.

"There are lots of other gods in the world," says Emory, "all claiming to be the One. The Buddhists rub the stomach of their little Buddha statues. You wouldn't want to do that with Jesus. You are full of questions, India!"

"Here's another," I say. "What's that dish of funny-colored muck?"

"Scrapings from a cut on one of our hound's feet," he answers. "In the scrapings are animalcula too small to see except with a special lens. They cause blood poisoning in a cut or burn."

I nod as if I understand.

Emory sees through me and grins. "Combinations of

different bread molds and fruit molds seem to kill those little animalcula," he says. "They are called bacteria. Certain molds seem to kill the bacteria or eat them, I am not always sure. I want to find out what and why and how it can be used to solve the great mystery of infections."

He guesses I don't understand and switches over to the more general. "You have been playing with white-trash boys at their games. I heard that on the grapevine. They want me to keep your nose in a book instead. Why don't you play with girls?" His eyes question me, and he rocks his skinny self back, hands in pockets, as if he already knows the answer.

"Girls are not nearly as much fun as boys. I like boys is all," I answer.

"What do you play with the boys?"

"War."

"Why?"

"Because it is what they play. If I wear trousers they let me be a soldier. We play the Battle of Manassas. Usually I am a private, but I get to hold the horses and go on raids."

"Horses?"

"They are . . . invisible."

Emory nods. "My brothers played games like that," he says. "My brothers are in the real war now. They are fools to join up."

Then he slaps down a notebook in front of me and takes on a churchy voice. "India, I am a tutor of physical philosophy at the University of Virginia. Until the war ends and school starts I am to be your teacher," he announces to me.

I feel my legs dangling from my chair like a little girl's.

"The following are our subjects." On a slate is written in my mother's hand, *Scriptures, household economics, handwriting, declamation.*

"We'll start on chapter one of *Mackey's Moral Behavior for American Girls*," Emory says.

On the table next to me is a brass tube with an eyepiece up top, eight inches long. It shines and sits aslant a black basalt stand.

"What's that?" I ask.

"It's called a microscope," says Emory. "I brought it back from the university. Now repeat after me," he says. "'A Godly life is a swift river which runs through the garden of temptation.'"

"'A Godly life is a swift river through the garden of temptation," I reel off.

"Which runs through," says Emory.

"What is the microscope for?" I ask.

"You can see tiny bacteria that are invisible to the naked eye," Emory answers. "'A Godly life is a swift river which runs through the garden of temptation.'"

"Can you show me? Can I look through it?"

"Let's get the prism out. It needs a prism to refract enough light for you to see." He turns the scope around, catches a ray of sunlight in the prism, and inserts a glass slide. "That is hog's blood," he says.

"It isn't red!"

"No. Neither is a cell of your blood under those lenses."

"What are those little things swarming through it?"

"Bacteria. Watch this." Emory takes the slide out and puts a drop of what smells like whiskey on the center. "Now look again."

"They've stopped moving!"

"Whiskey kills them. So does flame."

"What's that over there?"

"Three samples of bread mold and fruit mold spores. 'A Godly life is a swift river which runs through the garden of temptation. How easy it is to gather its blossoms. How sweet they smell. But we must not' . . . Repeat after me, India."

"What is that big book? What does that gold writing say?"

"It's in German. It's a book on plant chemistry."

I slide it off the shelf. "Can you read German?"

"Of course. Greek, Latin, and French, too. I had to read them all before even matriculating at the university. Please, India . . . 'A Godly life' is what?"

"What would happen if I put a hair from my head under the lens of the microscope?"

Emory taps his teeth with his pencil. "All right, we'll look. But then we're supposed to finish this essay on resisting temptation and you're supposed to write it out from memory in perfect spelling and handwriting."

Under the lens, the hair looks like a rose twig. Emory lets me compare it to a horsehair. We look at a berry skin and a drop of water, then a cactus spine.

"What is that?" I ask, pointing to a flask with a heavy glass stopper and a skull and crossed bones on the label.

"Nitric acid," he answers.

"And what is it for?"

"Look." He takes off his ring. "This ring is twenty-four-karat gold," says Emory.

I examine the ring. It is a wide-banded man's ring and has double teardrop stones in a figure eight.

"If you want to test for gold," he says, and reaches for the flask, "touch the metal with a stopper of nitric acid. If the metal is pure gold it will remain unchanged. All false gold contains copper. If the ring is false gold, nitrate of copper will form in the liquid."

His ring and the solution remain clear.

I open a book on cactuses. "If you let me borrow it," I say, "I will memorize all about these plants instead of the Godly river. They won't know."

Emory squirms in his chair. "That book is a botanists' *Guide to Succulent Plant Chemistry*. Girls aren't supposed to read chemistry or botany. Lots of men say they can't use it in life, and it hurts girls' minds to think like men."

"Do you believe that?" I ask him.

He toys with a pencil and then meets my eyes. "No. Not

for a second do I believe that, but shut your mouth, India Moody, or they'll take you right away and pack you off to a convent school and then where'll you be?"

"Supposing this?" I tell him. "When science commences to hurt my mind, I'll scream, and then we can stop and go back to the Godly river."

How God Made
the World

It is almost Christmas, months since Pa left home. He gets a fortnight's furlough and takes me hunting over near Front Royal. We set out at five in the morning, December 24, 1861. He has promised Christmas turkeys to Geneva Trimble.

"Is the war almost over, Pa?" I ask.

He shakes his head.

"Why not? Everyone says we're wearing out the Yanks."

"Who says?"

"The papers say the Yanks are near licked. All the ladies in the Virginia Ladies Aide say so, too. Mama makes me go every week to the meetings. We make lint and roll bandages. I hate it. I'd rather put on trousers and be in the war fighting Yankees."

"India, why do you take on so?"

At the top of a hill Pa stands still and aims. He fires, and we have our first turkey.

Then he tells me, "It's all going to start up next year.

Nothing's happening except both sides getting ready. Listen a little minute," says Pa. "What do you hear?"

"Nothing."

"It's too warm for December," Pa says. "It feels like the last seconds before a thunderstorm." He reloads his gun and slings the turkey into a sack. "Look at the sky. Dead quiet. I have nerves, India. Nerves like an old granny."

"Maybe it will come up a storm, Pa. Maybe you hear it hours off, like a horse."

Pa shakes me off. "Pussy Willow, we are in a pocket of time just before God's terrible tempest breaks over us."

"Back in the summer you said the Yanks would all go home for haying in October," I reminded him. "That they all signed up for a three-month run."

"It was true," Pa answered. "But now Lincoln has four hundred thousand more troops. General McClellan's sitting in his tent just north of Richmond teaching every Massachusetts mother's son the art of war."

The number four hundred thousand is too much for both of us. We walk on through the dried jimsonweed. The sun comes up and Pa makes a fire for breakfast. "Four hundred thousand Yankee men, looking good and good-looking. Every last one thanking his lucky stars God's on his side."

"What do you mean, Pa? God's on our side."

"I don't think God's about to take a side, India. Seems

He's going to let the Yanks tear Virginia to pieces. Slavery has always been there for them that can afford servants. I never thought of it much before, 'cept I turn the other way if there's a slave auction going. Now I know better."

"How do you know better, Pa?"

"They say one in twenty Virginians ever owns a slave, but big bad slavery's down to Carolina and Mississippi on the cotton plantations. Some of the men talk what's called traitor talk. It's the thoughtful men who've been to school and such, the ones who've seen some of life. They say we all are going down on slavery's ship."

I didn't want to hear any idea that allowed a single blemish on the Southern cause.

I tell him then, "Emory Trimble is teaching me about mold and bacteria."

"What in thunder is that? Bacteria?" Pa stops. "Mama said you were learning your Scriptures and your household mathematics."

"Emory has a microscope," I tell him. "He brought it home from the university. The Trimbles have asked a visitor to stay for Christmas week. I call him Doctor Germany because that's where he's from. He's brought with him an even more powerful microscope. It is made of brass with lenses on each end. You can see things invisible otherwise."

"What do you mean 'invisible otherwise'?"

"Tiny animals you can't see even with a reading glass.

Bacteria, animalcula. For instance when you've sliced off a piece of fresh ham? Those little tiny bacterium fleas get on the edge of the knife and jump around, and if you don't kill 'em they cause the ham to rot. If you kill them with a splash of hard cider or fire they die. I have seen this happen, Pa. All day I look at blood drops and leaf parts and every old thing. You see inside stuff. You see how God really made the world. He gave us a million cells, and in each one he put a million bugs bumping into each other. Emory says so and I have seen it with my own eyes. Emory says he will be the American doctor who takes medicine out of the dark ages and into the light, and I intend to help him do it. "

"India!"

"Is this wrong to talk about, Pa?"

He does not answer me but tears a piece off a rasher of side meat, twirls it around a stick, and puts that and a biscuit over the fire. "First you start playing boys' games with a lot of village ruffians. Two shakes after that you abandon your regular lessons and start learning men's science."

Pa knows I won't stop, and I know he won't tell Mama about it.

"Pa?" I ask, turning my bacon stick thoughtfully. "You know what I do sometimes?"

"What, India?"

"Sometimes, when I'm alone, I imagine where you must be. Riding up strange roads. Eating out in the dark. I pray

to Jesus, Pa. I pray to him to take care of you. But sometimes I think those prayers don't reach God's ears at all. I
think they just fall through the leaves in trees over where
you camp. Do you hear my prayers falling on you mixed up
with the rain?"

Pa stamps out the fire. He packs breakfast away and lets
me carry the turkey. "I hear you every morning before I open
my eyes, or I would not be able to get up," he answers. "Oh,
India," Pa goes on, "I don't guess I belong in this war."

"Why, Pa?"

He turns his face from me. "They gave me a pistol. But I
can't kill," he says with such shame.

DOCTOR GERMANY

To the Trimbles' Christmas comes a neighbor, Mr. David Hunter Strother. He is a boyhood friend of Tom Trimble, but now he is a Virginia Yankee man. There aren't many Virginia Yanks, I can tell you. No one wants to hear about why he joined the Union Army, because it could cause a huge fight on Christmas Day. Mr. Strother does not wear his Yankee uniform.

He is an accomplished gentleman with perfect manners, David Strother. He has presented Geneva with a small sketch portrait of herself that he drew last summer in colored chalks.

Then he plays "The Holly and the Ivy" on the grand piano in the parlor. He sits down on the piano bench, raising the tails of his coat, and skims a hand admiringly across the gold word BECHSTEIN that decorates the soundboard. David Hunter Strother plays the piano like an angel from heaven.

Geneva is happy to let the Spreckle sisters twitter away

harmlessly as turkey is served. Both sisters are in love with the South's great hero, Captain Turner Ashby. We have seen his portrait in the Winchester newspaper. Turner Ashby, with his long eyelashes, is the Lord's personal gift to the Southern cause. He skips through bullets that assail him like hailstones and emerges to fight another day, unhurt as if by magic. Ashby has become a legend, like a knight of King Arthur's round table.

"I, for one, would give every stick and tick of my possessions to ride with Turner Ashby," I announce.

"You will not speak like that, India," cuts in Mama. "You will remember you are a young lady. You will mind your manners."

No war talk invades the Christmas dinner. Only the animalcula come up. Doctor Germany spells it out for us. He tells everyone at the table that American doctors north and south are simpletons. At his university in Germany, he teaches doctors to wash their hands before operating on patients. If this were done, if instruments in their bags were cleansed in boiling water, their patients would live instead of dying of infections.

"Tell about the drinking water, sir," I pipe up.

Doctor Germany swallows and says, "Perfectly right. A curious young lady who seems to know something of science."

Mama flashes me a look.

Thousands of soldiers' lives could be saved, Doctor Germany tells us, if the drinking water and army food were not infected with trillions of these bacteria. Doctor Germany cuts his Christmas dinner up precisely and speaks to the slices of turkey on his plate. "The horses . . . what is the polite word? They foul the streams and the men drink thereof. Presto! Half the troops are doubled over with dysentery."

To Doctor Germany's left is Doctor Junius Hooks. His face gets purpler by the minute. No one knows who to believe, Doctor Germany, who has insulted American medicine and talks to his dinner, or Doctor Hooks, who doesn't like to have anyone knowing anything important but him.

"Let's have a prayer of thanks for that wonderful Captain Turner Ashby," the Spreckles say, interrupting Doctor Germany. You would think the sisters were preparing to meet Captain Ashby the very next hour.

Turkey is cleared away and on comes Christmas pudding with hard sauce. Calvin asks all of us to sing "O Come All Ye Faithful."

Geneva Trimble's intent sits up square in her eyes. She sings the old carol with rage. Into her voice flows fear. It gleams in her eyes. She sings as if she could, all by her own self, push the war away. I cast my glance down in embarrassment for I have looked into the privacy of her heart.

Angry voices float in from the veranda. There is a spat

starting between Tommy Trimble, Emory's year-younger brother, and David Strother, the Virginia Yankee man.

I hide behind an aspidistra plant on the veranda. I want to hear the Yankee man tied in knots.

Strother jabs his finger in Tommy's breast. His voice is iron hard. "Do you know what big field gang slavery is, Lieutenant Trimble? Blacks down in the Delta get worked and whipped till they drop dead. Pregnant women. Children. It's a disgrace. The war's about *slavery*, Tommy. Ugly, godless, cruel slavery! Not about Yankees trampling our corn. Slavery is a cancer, and it must be cut out."

Tommy ignores this. Polite Virginians actually prefer the word *servant* to *slave*. The newspapers call slavery *Our Peculiar Institution*, or sometimes *The Southern Way of Life*, but we all know what they mean by that.

Tommy has a bad cold and his plum-red nose is running. He puts a preserved fig into his mouth and swallows it whole.

"Without our slaves there would be no one to work the fields, Strother, you know that. How in God's name are you going to run a country without field hands. Answer me that?

Strother glares and whispers, "You could pay them, for a start, Tom. And free them and educate them as they are children of the Lord the same as you and me.

Tom Trimble bolts a glass of claret. "Slavery is a natural

condition of certain classes of mankind," says Tommy. "Even the Greeks and Romans had slaves. It's in the Bible, for pity's sake, David! What is so different now?"

Finally Tommy asks, "Gonna wear the Yankee blue, David? Gonna kiss Mr. Lincoln's behind?"

Strother yanks Tommy gently by the sash of his belt. "Look backward into your parlor, Tom, my friend," Strother whispers. He turns Tommy's head firmly by the jaw. "See those good folks singing? See those faces so dear to you? Remember it well, because you will never see it again."

"Judas words!" Tom answers. His face goes serious after a gulp of claret. "And a traitor to Virginia and its people and soil!"

David Strother's complexion reddens darkly at the insult. With both hands under the armpits, he picks up Tom Trimble and begins to shake or throttle him, I cannot tell which.

Strother spits his words. "You and your stupid cause," he says. "Your cause is the enslavement of human beings. That's what your cause is!"

"The war is not over slavery," sputters Tom. "It is about the preservation of our way of life. The North wishes to destroy us and everything my father and your father have built here in the South!" His eyes flash and he shoves Strother's hands back away. "Your father would roll over in his grave if he saw you take sides against your own people, David!"

"You leave my father out of it, Trimble," Strother roars. He hits Tom with a huge slap in the face, bumping over his claret glass, which smashes on the floor.

At the sound of the breaking claret glass I rush terrified into my pa's lap.

The light in the parlor is gold, darkening to amber by the minute. A single finger of ruby sun stripes down the body of the corner clock. I have seen menacing eyes like Strother's one other time. They were the eyes of a slit-eyed stray bulldog who almost bit off Eddie's fingers.

Strother, with a sweaty, jumpy hand on the front doorknob, remembers to thank Geneva with a stiff bow and wish her a Merry Christmas, as if nothing had happened. Geneva storms onto the veranda. My head on Pa's shoulder, I watch Tommy Trimble catch brimstone from his mama for starting a fight with a guest on Christmas Day.

Emory chimes in and tells Tommy to stay off the subject of our Southern way of life, especially when Ester is in the kitchen. Tommy brushes off his tunic sleeves where Strother grabbed him.

The youngest Trimble brother, Rupert, is a cadet at Virginia Military Institute. He has drunk entirely too much mulled wine and grins at Tommy around his mother's bulk.

Geneva yanks the shoulder tabs of Tommy's uniform. "Get yourself into the house and into bed or I'll pull off your looey stars and send them back to your captain," she threatens. Tommy's answer dissolves in a spasm of coughs.

Doctor Germany puts his ear against Tommy's chest. He gets out something he calls a stethoscope . . . this is an India rubber tube connected to a steel cone. Off the cone run two rubber hoses up to his ears. Doctor Hooks has never seen a stethoscope and looks at Doctor Germany peevishly.

Doctor Germany slips the listening cone under Tommy's shirt and hears Tommy's heart beat and his lungs breathe right through the skin and ribs.

"You have pleurisy rales, young man, and a fever," says Doctor Germany. He instructs Tommy to sleep in his brother's humid glass house, to drink weak tea by the liter, and not to move from his bed for ten days. He reaches into his vest pocket and produces a dozen tiny pills that rattle around in a tin box. "These Salicin pills may help. They are better than quinine in the bloodstream. Take one in the morning and one at night without fail," says Doctor Germany.

Doctor Hooks wants to apply hot cups to Tommy's back and bleed the ill humors off. Doctor Germany calls "bleeding off" medieval nonsense and pats Doctor Hooks on the back. He then tells Tommy slavery is also medieval nonsense and to go to bed, taking the pills until they run out.

Maybelle pulls our wagon home. We ride, singing "Good King Wenceslas" to the pastures of dozing sheep. Beady mouse eyes shine out from between the dry corn shocks. They are shrewy and smart like David Strother's. I am afraid that David Strother's voice contains the truth of the Northern side, and that truth is as cold and permanent as the planets.

"Pa," I say.

Pa pulls me into the driver's seat. He holds his arms around my waist on the rest of the way home. "What is wrong with my Pussy Willow?" he asks.

"I don't like Mr. David Hunter Strother," I say, pouting.

"Strother has the worst temper in the whole valley," says Pa. "He once shot his own horse in the head for throwing him."

"I don't like what he says," I tell Pa.

"He should not have lost his temper with Tom," Pa agrees. "Even if he is right, he shouldn't have hit Tom like that."

"What do you mean 'right'?" I ask. "I hate what he says about . . . about the South and the cause and all. It's a lie!"

Pa's eyes follow the up-and-down rhythm of Maybelle's rump. "The trouble is, what Strother says is true, my love. It is why God will allow the North to win."

"Then don't be a soldier, Pa! Don't! Don't go back!" I say. I pound him on the chest with my fists. But we both know that once in the army you can't get out. There is no quitting or hiding. Deserters are found by the Home Guard, arrested, and thrown in prison. Even when the war is done, a deserter will be stained with shame for the rest of his days.

"I promise, promise, promise I will be good and not say anything mean or critical if we can hide at Uncle Peter and Aunt Divine's in Kettletown. The Home Guard will never find you there, Pa. You can help Uncle Peter with his farm. We can wait until the war is over! I promise to be good!"

The wheels of our wagon bump. Maybelle strains to pull us over the dry mud tracks along the road to home. She flicks her tail, and it brushes just the top of my head. Mama sits in the back of the wagon, holding a sleeping Eddie in a blanket, pretending not to hear us. Pa grabs me with his one big hand over my two wrists and holds them down.

"Hush! You will upset your mother," he whispers.

Mark of Honor

New Year's Day 1862 feels warm as the first of May. I bring in wood for the cookstove, stuff it in, light it, and begin to make breakfast. By the sound of Pa's movements upstairs, I can tell whether he is putting on his home clothes or his soldier clothes. Now it is soldier clothes, and my heart slips down a little from its usual place.

Pa is not a good-bye-saying man. Instead of saying he must leave, he says he has something for me in his tunic pocket.

It is a letter from Julia, the first mailed letter I have received in my thirteen years on earth. I hold the envelope against my heart, as if it might burn up unread at any moment.

"The letter was sitting in the post office yesterday," says Pa. "See, it is postmarked November but didn't come in until the Christmas mail. You know the Yanks disrupt our mail. They throw it in ditches."

I examine the stamp and the Ohio postmark. The light

of the seven o'clock sky springs through the front window and frames Pa's face in a perfect square. Things like sun and seasons are the same as ever they were. All else in the world is changed since the war. I smooth out the envelope with Julia's familiar handwriting on it.

"Why, Pa? Why ruin the mail for ordinary people?"

"You are forever asking me questions I cannot answer," says Pa.

"It is so cruel to ruin people's letters. Supposing I were a child waiting to hear from a lost mama or papa. Supposing—"

Pa interrupts me. "The Union wants to make us suffer. They believe if the people suffer, somehow we will have the strength to bring down the Confederate government. Stupid! Common people have no strength to bring down governments."

"We should do it back to the Yankees!" I say angrily. "We should take all their horrible Yankee mail and burn it in a big bonfire."

"There is enough suffering," says Pa with a small sigh. "God may hear and turn your wish against you, India."

"Yes, Pa," I grumble, but I don't mean it.

Pa gives me two pennies for postage stamps so that I may write back to Julia. I never get money otherwise. Mama holds our money and hides it where only she knows. Pa gives Mama his pay envelope when he is home. His pay is not in federal dollars but Confederate money. Mama says Confederate dollars are not worth the paper they are printed on.

"Try and give the letter to somebody going to Harpers Ferry," Pa says. "You'll get it in the Yankee mail then and it will go on the train to Ohio." Pa takes a biscuit out of the stove and listens for Mama waking upstairs, but we hear nothing. "Your mama was praying for hours last night," he tells me. "Praying Captain Davis takes me into the quartermaster's corps and lets me run the ambulances and the supply wagons."

"Will they take you, Pa?"

"I'll find out when I rejoin the regiment today."

"What happens if they don't?" My voice prickles with low panic.

Pa does not answer right away. He is preparing what he will say to me while he bites into his biscuit and drinks acorn coffee. "Can't kill a fly, that's me," he says. He makes a mean face at the bitter green coffee.

"The army is full of decent church-raised men," he explains, tired eyes on the embers of the stove fire. "The Bible says, 'Thou shalt not kill.' So after the first time they kill they get nervous tics and nightmares. They are murderers suddenly. The memory of those killings will stay all sealed up in their minds for the rest of their days. I can't do it, India. I can't even shoot the Yankee horses, Pussy Willow."

"It is so cruel to make the poor horses suffer."

Pa agrees. "Cruelty," he says, "leaves the taste of sickness in the mouth."

"But *they* are the cruel ones," I argue. "The Yankees."

Pa shakes his head. "It is both sides the same. Last week the Winchester paper wrote that whoever wins this war will get to write the history books their way. The paper said whatever side wins will tell its own side's story and all the grandchildren and great-grandchildren down the years will believe that version of it."

"And you, Pa?" I whisper.

Pa touches the pistol that sits in a hard leather holster on his belt. The holster belt creaks when he stands. He says, "I do neither good nor harm. I would like to do some good, so I hope they take me in the quartermaster's corps. I can handle horses and harness as well as any man in the army."

He wipes his mouth on his sleeve. The gold braid is no longer shiny but brown and tattered. I put my arms around him and lock my hands in the small of his back.

"Don't pull me back, my sweet one," he says. "To be held in this way by you and your mama is a torture."

I let him go and hear him steal out into the yard, where he swings into the saddle and rides up the street away before Mama wakes. There are a hundred things I forgot to tell him. A hundred things I want to ask him. I want to hear him humming as he stitches a new set of traces. "Will that ever come again or is this the new way?" says a voice inside me. Because I am afraid of the answer, I follow him down to Buckmarsh Street to catch a last glimpse of him. Then I cry, standing in the street like a child with a skinned knee.

Julia's Christmas letter waits like a small live thing in my pocket. I want to hurry through my chores so I can read it over and over again and think about what I will write back. It will be my sixth letter to Ohio since Julia left last summer. Who knows how many she has received?

Already I know my answering letter to her will be proper, containing nice things I have been taught to say, because my words will be passed from hand to hand in the Pardoe family and read aloud.

I will try to write cheerfully. I will tell Julia that Pa will be home soon. That he is proudly serving and was feeling fine at Christmas. I will not write that Mama cries herself to sleep every night and I block my ears not to hear it. I will write that Christmas at the Trimbles' was a grand affair with every delicacy on the table. I won't say that we have almost no sugar, salt, coffee, cloth, ink, needles, or anything else at all because of the Yankee blockade of all goods to the South.

I tear open the letter before Eddie wakes and wants his breakfast. Julia may not be able to multiply five times seven, but she writes an elegant hand. Her letter paper is Parthenia's cream note paper that comes in a blue box from France. I run my fingertip over the tiny words PARIS, FRANCE blind stamped on the inside flap of the envelope.

Julia writes that more than a hundred boys from Oberlin College have signed up in the Ohio regiments to fight for the Yankees. Alden will be recruited by the Union Army if there is a military draft in Ohio. I shudder reading this. Alden might-could come back down to Virginia and shoot my pa because they were in different uniforms. "Luckily," Julia says, "Northern boys who have the money can buy out of the army and pay a poor boy to serve in their place for $300." By these words I know Mr. Pardoe has already paid to keep Alden in soft civilian shoes.

"I swallow hard, dear India," writes Julia using pig latin, "because the am-day college takes as many women as men. Can you imagine! Why didn't we go to Athens and Ohio University, which is only open to men? I am afraid Mother may cause me to do college preparatory studies. This means dratted Latin, even Greek! As you know I never mastered long division and cannot keep a single Latin declension or the names of the continents in my head! So I will fail to qualify. You should come here, India, for they have men and women students who milk cows and thresh hay at the Oberlin farms and thus pay their tuition fees. You could conjugate French verbs and do trigonometry tables all day, m'dear, and birth litters of piglets at night!"

Mama comes downstairs with a bitter face because Pa has said his good-bye with only a brushing of the lips unfelt in her sleep. Tracks have appeared between Mama's mouth and nose that were not there last summer. I feed Eddie his breakfast and then Grandpa Moody his. Both of them fuss at me. I get Grandpa Moody to sing "The Sweetest Story Ever Told" so Eddie'll eat up his egg.

Mama spends the morning hiding everything valuable under a board in the stable floor. It takes her close to an hour to pry the board up and then to dig a hole under it. . . . Into the hole tumble her silver teapot, six spoons, my gran's wedding ring, an enameled thimble, a diary, expensive harness brasses from Pa's shop. "The Yankees won't find that," says Mama. But I don't know if the Yankees would care for thimbles.

"I want to go now," I tell Mama when my morning work is done.

"Where? Where are you going?" Mama asks. She does not like anyone going anywhere. When I leave, Mama says, she is set upon by hives until I return.

"Mama, please." I try and catch her attention, but she is always darting her eyes down the street or in the corners of the room. The day is so warm I could lean back on the air.

"I need you. I need you here with me," says Mama.

"I want to run!" I say. "It feels like spring. I want to run and run!"

"You are like an ungovernable boy!"

"I don't care, Mama! I *am* like a boy. Maybe I should have been one."

"Don't you go wandering up to the Trimble place," says Mama, lips pursed. "You don't bother them New Year's Day. You leave them alone!"

Then we hear it. It is a slow increasing rumble, at first like the distant chattering of birds, then a tumbling of enormous boulders. We see them, under a red-brown cloud of dust on the very end of the road coming up toward town. It is Stonewall Jackson's brigade, and they are marching through the valley on their way north to some mysterious destination.

Where is the army going? We don't know.

"Into western Virginia or Pennsylvania where they've got no business," sniffs Mama. She gathers Eddie into her tendon-tracked arms. We watch the army pass right in front of our front door. The dust that comes along with them will have to be cleaned off every surface in the house.

"We might just see Stonewall himself!" I chirp, hoping to lighten her.

"We'll never see him," says Mama. "They hide him among the other officers. That's why he rides that little shrimp of a sorrel mare. They're afraid of spies," she explains. "They're afraid a saboteur is hiding in one of the houses on Buck-marsh Street and will assassinate General Jackson, so they surround him and give no target."

Mama pulls me and Eddie slowly back from the edge of the front step of our house. The other Berryville families have come to their windows or doorways. It's mostly women and children, now that the men are in the army. Of course there are the old men with bad eyes and the trembles. The old men sit around the general store and talk about Indian wars that they served in. You hear them in the evenings. They whittle bits of wood and smoke and wish they were young enough for this war.

There are the boys, like Frawley Turpin, who play make-believe soldier. Today the boys, all smooth cheeks and clean hair, are openmouthed at the frightening force of the genuine army.

Suddenly I see General Stonewall Jackson for just a minute. A slice of a view between other jostling officers, of a furry-bearded man, thin as a beanpole, with colorless eyes that seem to be gazing into a distance that no one else can see. He is mounted on a stumpy little red mare. Then the other officers close around him and I see just tramping men again. "It was General Jackson just a minute ago," I say.

Mama looks for him but doesn't find anyone measuring up to General Jackson's fame and glory. She says with a little respect, "Your father reports General Jackson is like a magical man in a circus. Your father says his eyes shine in the dark and he sucks lemons all day to ward off disease."

I see nothing more of Stonewall or the astonishing Turner Ashby. I see only men so skinny a good wind could blow them away. "Look at that one," says Mama. "No shoes, feet as black as a leper's. They are ragtag as a bunch of beggars."

I smell the army as it goes by. It is a hard, dirty smell. It is awful to breathe it in. I turn my head and cover my nose and mouth with my apron, frightened by this foul odor. We wait to see if Pa comes by and is among the troops somewhere. We see men who look almost to be Pa and then dissolve into someone else entirely.

A hand waves. It is Lieutenant Tommy Trimble at the

head of his unit, riding his favorite gelding, Othello. Tommy is red in the face with excitement. He and all the rest of the soldiers have stripped their uniforms down to shirtsleeves, as if we have a summer's day.

"Hallo, Moodys! Good news for you!" Tommy shouts. He stops and pulls over a minute before heading out with his troops. "Cy Moody has been assigned to the quartermaster's corps, this morning," he tells us. "He wanted me to get word to you. He's leading six ambulances and the supply wagons way behind us."

The lines that I hate so much relax around Mama's mouth. She bends forward and sobs with gladness into her hands. I hold Eddie. Tom Trimble's eyes have already left us. They are searching the horizon, north of town. Somewhere up there the war awaits Tommy, full of adventure, full of glory.

"Keep my brother Emory out of trouble!" Tom Trimble says to me. He chucks me under the chin. The easy carriage of his young mounted body, holding his reins in one casual hand, is like the picture of *Our Virginia Hero*, going to battle, in the Winchester newspaper. Tommy has figured out how to be that hero, I tell myself. In a moment he and his unit are swallowed up by the road ahead and the hundreds of marchers tramping behind them. Behind the steeple of the Presbyterian church the sun slides quickly down the winter sky. The afternoon turns smartingly cold.

Mama's voice is light now. She gives Eddie a kiss and

touches my shoulder. "Go in," she says. "Play with Eddie and his building stones. Make some coffee, and keep yourself warm. I am going to wait for Pa."

I pile a tower of Eddie's stones on the floor and let him chew one of Pa's leather toys. I bring a blanket out for Mama, then a cup of acorn coffee. It is too dark to see Pa, but Mama is sure he is there somewhere in the moving carpet of men. A wagon goes by and then another. If Pa is among them inside the grayness there is no sign. Sleet spits down, and Mama comes in to get warm. We bow our heads in solemn prayer at supper and thank the Lord for Pa's more certain safety among the wagons and the wounded.

A branch outside my bedroom window wakes me in the hours before dawn. Its ice-coated twigs tap like mice feet on the glass. I wrap myself in a coverlet and go downstairs. A can of milk sits almost frozen on our back step. I put more wood into the stove's embers to warm the milk. Silently I sit in the dark kitchen, writing to Julia in my head.

"Pa is going to be safe in his new corps, we hope and we pray," I will tell her first. How can Julia understand this? Her father comes home from his law office every evening. He removes his beautifully polished shoes and sits down with a glass of sherry brought by a servant who is better fed and paid than any man who marched up our street today.

Suddenly our front door bursts open. I think for a minute it is the wind but it is Pa himself. He can just see me by the stove's winking little flames. Easing himself into Grandpa

Moody's rocking chair, Pa takes off his pistol and slings it on the table, shoving it away from himself.

"What are you doing up this late, Pussy Willow?" he asks me.

"I am writing to Julia in my head," I say. "There is no oil for the lamp. No candles in the house." I throw myself in his lap. "I didn't think I'd see you till your next leave . . . not till maybe Easter," I blurt out.

"The roads are frozen mud," he says. "The wagons are up to their axles. We can't move."

"Can you stay the night? Can you stay for breakfast? We have sausage!"

Pa holds me by the shoulders and smooths back my hair. "Tom Trimble is dead," he says.

"Tom Trimble! Tom was just . . . just this afternoon outside in the street! How is he dead? He talked to us! It can't be, Pa! Did the Yanks shoot him?"

"There was an ice storm," says Pa. "Tom had no coat. Nothing. He started a high fever, and I guess his lungs filled up. He could not draw breath, and he just died. Calvin and Emory rode all the way over from Longmarsh. They found me and made me take them to Tom's unit with brandy and a blanket and a winter coat for Tom. We were too late. Tom died coughing in his father's arms. I had to dose Calvin with the brandy. I thought he would go mad."

Pa watches slush trickle off the soles and heels of his boots into a puddle before the stove. "Tom asked if his brother would shoot him past the cheek . . . so that he would have a mark of honor lying in his coffin."

"A mark of honor?" I ask.

"He was ashamed to die of pneumonia. Ashamed. He wanted to die of a bullet wound if he was to die at all. Emory wouldn't do it. The sergeant refused to do it. I had to do it because it was his last wish."

"You!"

"I let the bullet graze past his cheek. The boy hardly shaved yet."

———————◆●◆———————

Frawley Turpin and friends circle Tommy's body, lying splendidly in its dress grays. Folded on the chest is the Bonnie Blue Flag. Along the right cheek is the crease of a bullet.

I turn from the casket and find Emory at the back of the room. Emory's voice seesaws, one minute angry, the next nearly weeping. "His sergeant told us Tommy started to shake during the ice storm," Emory tells me. "We got three overcoats on top of him. Didn't matter a bit by the time we got there. It was too late," he repeats and swallows. "I had no medicine to give him. Tom should be upstairs in his bed this very minute on sick leave. Instead he's downstairs in his casket, a fool for the cause."

I don't ask why there's a bullet bruise on Tommy's face because I know. For the benefit of others, the Spreckle sisters tell all later in the parlor, "Tom Trimble was the first to die in this New Year. You can see the mark of the Yankee bullet as it hit his cheek." The sisters do not question that this is not a mortal wound. They do not seem to know that there was no battle for Tom to die in.

In the parlor of Longmarsh Hall the minister's wife goes quietly from one to another mourner. She spots whoever is weeping, then she collects the tears from the eye in a tear vase. Later the finger-size vase will be corked, sealed, and given to Geneva as a keepsake. I swear a silent oath that whatever may come my way in life no tear of mine will go in a little vial to be mixed with other tears.

I go to Emory's glass house and let myself in. Through its windows I see the surrounding orchards, trees bare, and the meadows brown. Frawley Turpin and dozens of boys from Berryville have escaped the funeral now. Galloping, bugle calling, the boys are away on their invisible horses into the hayloft of the Trimbles' barn, playing war.

Emory comes suddenly into the room. He closes the door firmly, clicking its latch on the houseful of mourning people, on his mother and father, who are sitting dressed in black in their bedroom, and on his brother, Rupert the cadet, who is trying to comfort them.

Emory sits on his leather-topped work stool and curses.

"Why are you so angry?" I say.

"My brother Tom fancied himself the Hero of the South," says Emory.

"You can't be angry at the dead," say I, "because they can't be angry back, because they can't be angry in the presence of God."

Emory draws a deep breath. "Good Presbyterian logic," he says, conceding my point. "It's the war that makes me angry, India. It wasted Tom's life. I only hope it's over before it claims Rupert, too. As for me, I have all the more reason now to devote myself to my discoveries," Emory says. "It's the only way to face tomorrow."

I wait for him to explain to me how this is to be.

"Whatever was in those little tablets from our Christmas visitor actually seemed to stop Tom's fever in two days. Then Tom refused to take more because he said he felt fine. It will take months to hear what they are concocted from. Our doctor friend has gone home to Germany."

"Are there pills left?" I ask. "Can you not look under the microscope and find out what they are made of?"

Emory laughs. He answers, "The microscope doesn't show how a compound is formulated. The heart of all trouble in science is that it takes a lifetime of waiting to gather information for research. It can take years for one doctor in one university to find out what has been discovered in another university. In the meantime medicine is practiced by blind sawbones who cause more disease than they treat."

"What can you do, Emory?" I ask.

"Study more," he says. "There is a secret somewhere in living matter and infected organisms. I know this much; disease is caused by bacteria in the blood. This is what causes gangrene in a wound. I suspect bacteria also cause typhoid, cholera, scarlet fever, dysentery, and pneumonia. I believe I can prevent gangrene by applying whiskey to a wound and to the instruments I use. I have done it on animals and on myself. But there must be some omnivorous substance in nature that can be used by mankind to devour disease in the bloodstream."

"What is 'omnivorous'?" I ask.

"Omnivorous is all-eating . . . all-consuming," answers Emory.

"And you will find this!" I say.

"I removed a little blood from my brother when he was ill. I looked at it under the microscope and compared it to my own healthy specimen."

"What did you see?"

"I don't know. Something different. If I had my microscope at the university, which is much more powerful, I might have known what it was. But on my brother's honor, India, I will solve this mystery."

I say, "You will be a famous man all over the world. I wish I could . . . I wish I could be a little part of it, too. I mean . . . with you, as your . . . assistant," I stutter.

Emory does not chuckle at me as I am afraid he will. "What do you know of science?" he asks.

I try to answer sensibly. I know nothing, of course, nothing I have not learned here. "I have . . . I have memorized the minerals you have in your collection."

"My rock collection? All of them?"

"All." I begin with chromium sulfate and manganese and go on through sulfur, copper oxide, aluminum, selenium, malachite. The names come easily. I name two dozen more.

Emory listens as if to a song. "That is perfect," he says. "Absolutely perfect. I know men in college who couldn't do that."

"I can name every plant in this room," I add. "Cypress fern, ferocactus, aloe, opuntia. I have been studying them after my chores. It's like memorizing a poem, really."

"A poem of chemistry, plant, and mineral."

Through the glass roof we can see the stars come out. "It is all I know of science," I say a little shyly. "Just what I've learned here. Except the names of the stars. Pa has taught me them."

"Name them!" says Emory. We both look up through the roof windows.

"Oh, there's the Pleiades over there, and Andromeda and Cassiopeia. There's Orion in the east. You can just see him."

"You know those are all part of the mythology of ancient Greece," Emory says.

"Yes, Orion is a hunter, ursa minor and major are bears. But that is not science."

Emory rubs a piece of ice-clear cryolite between his palms like an amulet.

"No. It is poetry," answers Emory.

NANCY BOY

In my hand are a dozen silver spoons so small a doll could use them. They are part of a set with ruby glass salt boats, which Geneva uses for special occasions. I polish the tarnish off them.

It is April 1862. Emory has stolen the spoons from his mother's cutlery chest and boiled them clean. Geneva cannot find her spoons anywhere. Emory only shrugs when she asks him where they are. I pretend not to hear.

We spoon up substances taken from all parts of the Trimbles' stables and place samples in egg cups. I label them. Fruit mold spores are added to these to see what happens.

Emory's biggest collection is his chemical lab. It has tubes and flasks, beakers, pipettes, and crucibles. The drawers are full of different minerals all labeled in his scrawly handwriting.

"I could spell those out in a right clear hand," I volunteer.

"Excellent!" he says. "You can be my official assistant. That is what assistants do."

The results of Emory's experiments fill volumes of notebooks. They sag the shelf down heavily over our table.

"Will it be easy to change what doctors believe?" I ask him.

"Not right away," says Emory. "In the end all changes are brought about by the young over the old stick-in-the-muds. The old doctors think they know what they're doing," says Emory. "They actually believe fevers are caused by miasmas and ill humors." He stops to see if I take this in correctly.

"Impure air? Is that it?"

"Yes, and the fumes of sewers and swamp gases. They believe blood poisoning can be cured by cupping and leeching the blood of the sick person. Same principal as letting steam out of a kettle, but it's letting blood out of a person. This is witch doctory. What doctors believe now, in 1862, is what they believed in 1462."

"And what will the cure be?" I ask.

"It will be some mold that kills the animalcula or bacteria that cause illness, infections, and so forth," he answers. "Once Father had a blister from new riding boots. The blister became infected from bacteria contained in stable dirt. He ran a terrible fever. Old Junius Hooks bled him off with leeches on the skin of his spine. A lot of good that did!" Emory says. "I put on red oak bark. It's an antiseptic. Father improved."

Emory has cultured a dozen kinds of mold spores from different fruits.

Custard cups sit on every surface in the room. We have collected bacteria from horse dung, swine offal, and the flesh of trapped game. "Some of these molds appear to kill bacteria," says Emory, "but which ones, and how could they be introduced into the human bloodstream without doing more harm than they cure?"

During the winter of 1862 I have learned the names and species of a hundred plants, but no household economics. I have learned much Latin and some Greek, but no Scriptures. I can identify thirty minerals and have grown a dozen crystals by myself, but I have not learned ladies' penmanship or the correct composition of thank-you letters.

I move easily in Emory Trimble's south-facing laboratory among the bread pans filled with cactus and mosses in bottle gardens. Five or six years Emory declares, given a good laboratory, is what it will take him to solve the mystery of fevers.

"Then will come the difficult part," Emory says.

"And what could be more difficult than that?" I ask.

"Getting other doctors to accept it," he answers.

Emory receives letters from places I can only imagine on the schoolroom globe. They are thick letters on heavy paper with peculiar handwriting and stamps.

Emory's green eyes look a far piece beyond our glasshouse windows. He says, "I heard a story once. It was about a secret city in Arabia. No one could get into the city, even though they tried to scale the walls and bore holes through. Inside the city was a light, and the man in the story could see the light glowing but he couldn't get to it."

"A secret city?" I say.

"Yes. The city might as well be the city of Medicine. I'm like that man who bores holes and can't get in. Right this minute, India, there are the cures for malaria, cancers, consumption, all pestilence, only we don't know them. Hidden. Just like the light in that city." He drums his fingers impatiently on his desk. "Doctors are way ahead of us in Europe. I want to bring their chemistry and their doctorship to America. We are almost there!" Emory says this over and over. "We are almost out of the dark ages. Believe me, India, everything will change after this stupid war."

I hear the excitement in his voice. It is so catching. "I want to do that, too!" I blurt out.

"You'll come with me, India," says Emory. He takes my hand in his, all the while staring out the window. I think he does not even realize he is holding my fingers.

We both know Emory's splendid scientific life is all laid out like a great big hallway runner rug. As for me, Emory and I pretend. We pretend anything can and will happen just around the corner from today. I know better. *Girls and women will live just a step up from a good hunting dog till the moon and sun change places in the sky* is what the whole world says.

I have to start somewhere, so I concentrate on chemistry

and Latin. These two things we learn in their fundamentals from a Latin grammar and Lavoisier's *Elements of Chemistry*.

In the glass house Emory brings out a square of silk in a color he calls mauve.

"This color was invented in an English chemical laboratory four years ago," he says. "A friend sent me a swatch of it from London."

Mauve is a pinkish purple of such delicacy I can only hold the silk square to the light and gaze at it. I have seen it only in petunias and stained-glass windows.

"To invent new color!" I say. "It's as if men are taking on the work of God!"

"The work of men is the work of God. It's all the same thing," says Emory. "It will make its inventor a small fortune, since all the ladies in Europe want their silks dyed with it. If I cared to make money I would start a dye factory and make this cloth by the bolt."

Before I can swallow the words I blurt out, "But I care to make money, Emory! Look at this Englishman. He doesn't stop at just memorizing chemicals. He actually did something that you can buy and sell."

I look down at the piece of silk. "I know you'll say this is foolishness." I look into his wondering eyes and blurt out, "Women can be rich if they marry the right men, but women can never actually make money themselves. Unless it's just a few dollars like my Aunt Divine who sews clothing."

"What would you do with the money if you were rich, India?" Emory asks without batting an eye at such a radical idea.

"You would laugh at me," I say.

"Try me," answers Emory. He busies himself with a flask of nitric acid. "Tell me what you would do with money if you were to make it," Emory says.

I have not the courage to say the words in case Emory tells me the word *no*.

"I am determined," I say.

"Determined for what?"

I hold my breath for an instant. Then I tell him. "I am determined to go to college," I confide, "and put all this to some use, as you are determined to do in medicine. There is a college in Ohio. Oberlin College. Alden Pardoe is in the first-year class. Oberlin accepts women. They allow you to work out your fees on the college farm," I say. "I have it all in a letter from Julia." I wait for the word *no*, but it does not come.

"We must prepare you to take the entrance examination," says Emory. "It is all memorization, and precious little application. Do you have any money at all? College costs money."

"No," I answer, "but I will find some if it is the last thing I do."

"I will help you," says Emory, "if I can."

He sets out a small beaker of nitric acid. In it he dips a silver salt spoon. It immediately dissolves. "Now we have silver nitrite solution," says Emory. He splits the solution into two more beakers and drops a copper penny into the first. The solution turns blue, and a silvery white material appears.

"How can that be?" I ask. "I don't believe in magic tricks. How can I know what is happening and understand why?"

"Chemistry is the effect of one substance on another," he says, riffling through the pages of one of his books. He finds what he is looking for and turns the book so that I can see the page. It is the list of known elements, fifty or more of them. Emory flicks at the list with his finger. "All matter is composed of elements. Elements are the pure substances. When you combine them you get compounds. Water is made of two gas elements, oxygen and hydrogen. There are the elementary solids, which include the metals and the pure earths, and the gases, like hydrogen. More are discovered every year. Here is an alphabetical list, India. Many men have tried to assemble them in a logical table. Someday some genius smarter than I will figure out how."

I say those wonderful names—copper, iron, chromium, phosphorous. I remember their abbreviations easily because I suddenly love them as I would beautiful toys. From aluminum to zirconium I say them aloud. "I will have them by heart in a week," I tell Emory.

"You absorb this quickly, India," says Emory, "more quickly than my first-year students at the university. I have only to put the page in front of you. What you need to do is make notes of exactly what this little experiment consists of. Lab notes. In that book up there are other experiments. We will do them all, and you will learn to keep a lab journal."

Ester raps on the door. There are guests for noontime dinner. Two officers from General Lee's staff are seated at the Trimbles' table. One of them is Jeb Stuart, the legendary cavalry officer. Stuart's beard is bushy and his hair is as long as a woman's. He has that foxy look that tells a girl she shouldn't be alone with him too long.

From over the dining-room mantelpiece Tommy Trimble's photograph stares down at our table, his face and uniform gray as sleet.

When we sit down Calvin flashes Emory a warning look. It says to show respect for the guests and not to make trouble. Jeb Stuart is a knight of General Robert E. Lee's round table, just like Colonel Turner Ashby and Stonewall Jackson. I can't wait to write to Julia that I actually sat at table with such a famous Southern hero.

Ester has a sweet ham coming up, and Geneva wants no scraps with General Robert E. Lee's staff officers. But Emory starts picking away at the officers over the soup.

"How many men are they losing to camp fever?" he asks.

The older officer answers reluctantly. "Too many. Some are slackers, but most are sick enough."

"You ought not to allow the men to tie the company horses near a source of drinking water when they encamp," Emory tells them.

"And where are you going to tie 'em?" Stuart asks. "Poor exhausted beasts need shade and water. They better-should go under the trees."

"Yes," says Emory, his voice picking up. "And the poor beasts use the river as they would a stable floor, sir. Their excrement is filled with bacteria that cause camp fever. Your men drink from the same water and they all get sick. General Lee and Jackson would save half their army if they would pay attention to this."

I bubble along, too. "He's right! He's right! Come look under the microscope!"

They ignore me.

Jeb Stuart answers, "Young man, you can't fight a war without horses. You can't encamp a company of soldiers without a source of water nearby and without watering the horses when you cool them off. We are country men and farm boys. A few horse apples won't hurt us."

"Exactly right," says Calvin. "Manure makes excellent fertilizer, my boy. If it were full of poisons, as you say, it would poison our cabbage and tomatoes in the garden."

"I didn't say poison. I said *bacteria*," explains Emory. "Horse dung mixed with soil enriches the soil and composts over time. It doesn't poison anything, because the bacteria die and become earth. But uncomposted horse dung infects drinking water immediately with bacteria that are harmful to the human gut. That's saying it so simply a child can understand it." Emory slams his knife on the table in disgust. "If you want to win the war you'll keep your army healthy!"

Stuart stares intently with light hazel eyes into the face of Tommy Trimble above the mantelpiece, as if maybe Emory instead of Tommy should be the dead one. It is clear that nobody around the table has ever heard the word *bacteria*. Stuart mutters something about nancy boys. Emory leaves the table. There is an uncomfortable silence. I ask the older officer what a nancy boy is.

But Stuart turns back to me and smiles broadly. He says, "Well, miss, it's a man who shakes and quakes like a girl at the littlest thing in the world." He sparkles and eats the last mouthful of ham on his plate.

"I'm a girl," I say. "And I don't shake and quake. I would shoot to kill a Yankee in cold blood before he laid a hand on me!" I know Colonel Stuart is not really answering my question, because I put my foot over the grown-up line.

"You are a good little Confederate lady!" says the colonel.

"A stouthearted Bonnie Blue Girl!" agrees Calvin. The static leaves the room like a wind dying down. Emory shuts himself away. Ester speeds out with a plate of corn dodgers.

"He is stirred up," whispers Calvin across the table, "because all the other young men are in it and he cannot go because he is weak-chested."

The men smoke Calvin's cigars out on the veranda. I don't dare go into the glass house while Emory is fuming. Geneva beckons to me. Once upon a time I fit into her lap. Now she pulls me beside her. She gives me a square from a bar of chocolate that Doctor Germany sent through the Yankee lines. I eat the square as if it were the last food on earth.

"Chocolate is a taste from long before the trouble began," Geneva says. She breaks off another square wrapped in spring-green foil and tucks it into my pocket. "This will make your mama's temper sweeter, India," she says. "You bring it to her. I'd give half a pound to my son in there if I thought it would do a smack of good."

"What is a nancy boy?" I ask her.

"Oh, just soldier talk, bad old soldier talk," Geneva answers.

"But what does it mean?"

But Geneva will not tell me. I figure it is safe to go back to my afternoon plant care. When I have removed the scale from a rabbit's-foot fern I move over to the chemistry side of the glass house and begin to mix iodine and zinc over a crucible. This provides a nice purple cloud of iodine vapor and I hope it cheers Emory up.

"What is a nancy boy?" I ask Emory.

Emory won't talk to me. He makes notes and slams book covers until he knocks two promising spore cultures all over the floor.

I tell him he can catch more flies with honey than vinegar.

Emory sits me down. "They have no respect for any living soul who doesn't wear a uniform," he says. "They were sneering at me because they think any man not fighting is laying up. So I will show them. I will single-handedly point the heads of the Confederate high command at this scandal about camp fever and drinking water until they listen."

"How?"

"I am accepting a commission as a captain in the medical corps."

I nearly drop the beaker of iodine. "You can't be in the service," I say. "Your asthma! I thought they wouldn't take you!"

"They'd take a carved wooden Indian this year," says Emory.

"But everything will come to an end if you go," I say before I know what I'm saying.

"I will be a noncombatant and quite safe," he answers.

I press back the tears rising up in my throat. "It doesn't matter," I say. "The war will go on and on, Emory. Everyone says when they run out of regular soldiers they'll start taking half-wits and jackleg preachers. Then the blind and the deaf and dumb. The whole army will sooner or later get killed. That's what everyone in the world says. You'll be killed in some awful way and all your work will disappear, as if it had never been done at all!" My mouth is dry as sand. "And I'll have to go back to . . . being a poky old girl. Back to being a girl who has to learn to sew and wear hoop skirts and write thank-you notes!"

What gives me away in my eyes? What spurts into my voice? Emory hears it. He makes me sit across the table from him and holds my hands down firmly, as if they might fly off like sparrows.

The air is rich around us with the warm breath of plants. Something that has no words that I know passes between Emory and me. It pumps through every vein in my body like electricity. I have not been taught the name for this. No one has ever mentioned in front of me that such things happen between people. Still, I know just what it is, as if it were as simple to recognize as water or gold.

First and Last Words

It is May 5 of 1862, the second summer of the war. Mama and I lean out the top half of our doorway, peering down Buckmarsh Street. I was not tall enough to do this comfortably last year. Now I rest my elbows on the sill. Berryville is a hive of gossip.

Is the war coming here? The boys say so. They are full of what's going to happen. I linger in front of our house, trying to be included among them. I try looking oh-so-I-don't-care at the same time.

Frawley Turpin says, "A whole company of Yanks're gonna retreat through Berryville tonight! Y'all ready for 'em?" The boys stand in a circle around Frawley. They toe their initials in the dust of the stable yard.

"We're going to get us a Yank," Frawley brags on.

I turn to him. "Just what do you mean by the word *get*, Frawley Turpentine?" say I.

"Not for girls to know," Frawley sasses back at me.

When I wear a dress or pinafore, the boys talk to me as if I were less than a snail. When I wear trousers and hide my hair under a cap, they call me Pretty Boy, but they talk freely. The boys curse and chew cattail punk cigars, as they believe the soldiers do. They imitate carefully the soldiers' poses they see pictured in the papers.

The papers don't tell you a thing you can take to the bank. Our town just waits to fill up with what's going to happen.

Mama and I go to the roof to see better. "Is that the artillery?" I ask. "Ours or theirs?"

Mama doesn't answer. She tilts her head, listening for more. Her eyes turn to me.

"We are going to be rich tonight, Mama!" I tell her. "The boys say the Yanks are dumping everything they own . . . all their commissary wagons have been stolen by our side and everything in them, too!" I tell her. "I'm going to get you Yankee coffee, Mama. Frawley says he's going to get a whole Yank!"

Mama gives me a pale smile at this. "Frawley Turpin hasn't seen his first Yank yet, India."

"No, but when that Yank goes by me he'll be sorry."

"Hush up, India," says Mama.

Our neighbors on both sides are standing at their highmost windows. They are listening to our conversation. Mama knows it.

Mama sends me downstairs to the cellar with Grandpa Moody and Eddie in case one or the other side's artillery blows a hole in the middle of Buckmarsh Street. She will come down soon, she promises, but I know Mama is waiting for our army to follow the Yanks through town. She is waiting to see the top of Pa's head.

In the cellar I put Grandpa Moody into a rocking chair as far from the coal scuttle as I can get him, so he won't cough. Then I take Eddie on my lap. Eddie wants me to sing "I Long to Hear My Mother Pray Again." He wants his bed. He wants to nurse at Mama, even though I think she should have given that up a year ago.

Eddie hears thundering in the sky. He knows it's not an electric storm. So does Grandpa Moody. He rocks his cellar chair experimentally, as if he might have forgotten how chairs work.

"That's the sound of guns," Grandpa Moody says suddenly, as if there's a much younger man inside his body.

"Oh, it's only coming up a thunderstorm, Grandpa Moody. Don't fret."

"No. It's not," he declares, as if he can see through the ceiling. "It's guns."

Somewhere nearby the air splinters with the sound of a shell exploding. Mrs. Dowd, our neighbor, comes pattering down our cellar stairs because the Dowds' house has no basement. "It's the Yanks!" she says. "That's their boots you hear pounding and slapping down the street. I can't look, I'm too scared!"

I hand Eddie off to her, change into boy's clothes, and slip out the back window. In the alley behind the house the boys are gathering.

Suddenly the Yanks are running for their lives right down the middle of Buckmarsh Street. Our army must be on their tails no more than a few minutes away. I cheer, as if I'm at a horse race. Union blue bedrolls and knapsacks bounce in every direction. Caps, coats, and trousers race by, all colored the indigo of deep night sky. The men inside these strange uniforms groan in fear like pigs on slaughter day.

Frawley's voice rings out, "Stonewall's comin' to git y'all! He's gonna wring yer necks and stick ya up the tail with his bayonet!"

In between the knots of running soldiers, our Berryville street boys strut and spit at targets.

The Yankee army smells different from ours. The soldiers have a city look to them, and you can't understand a word they say.

I grab a knapsack that falls my way. I take another and another until my arms are full, and I rush to stash the bags safely through the cellar window of our house.

From every doorway children have sprung into the street like mice spilling from a grain shed. Six full knapsacks sit in our basement. What is in them I don't know. Suddenly, quickly as they came, the Yanks are gone and the street is silent.

I fall asleep, not remembering to take my clothes off. At midnight I hear Pa in the darkness somewhere. I hear his voice as I might in a blanketed winter dream. But I come awake suddenly because I must plug my ears with my fingers for the noise.

Three wounded Virginia soldiers have been brought into our house. By the staircase is a boy about a year older than me. Someone's tied his left wrist to the railing. His thumb is gone. He cries and thrashes like an animal with a broken back.

Doctor Hooks wears one of Mama's aprons, the front splattered red. Only then do I recognize Pa. He has lost twenty pounds of sow belly, as Mama always calls it. "Pa!" I cry. He cannot hear me for the howling of the wounded men.

He and Doctor Hooks have just laid a second soldier on the carpet. The soldier frowns, as if he were studying. His face is the color of candles.

Mama has strapped and buckled soldier three to our kitchen table with some of Pa's harness traces. Soldier three is a big man. He cannot move except his head, which he swings to one side and then the other like a clock pendulum.

Pa sees me. He shouts and holds out his arms to gather me in. I still can't hear anything but I can read his lips. "Go upstairs, Pussy Willow! You must not see this."

"Stay here!" orders Doctor Hooks. "We need her. She better-should learn this nursing work anyhow. It's what women do."

Mama calls from the kitchen, "India, take this!" She hands me a bottle of brown liquid. "Squirt a dropper in the boy's mouth. The one on the stairs. Get it into him!"

I try. He seems to choke on the first swallow. Some goes in. The rest dribbles down his chin.

The man on the kitchen table makes a terrifying effort to burst through his bonds and almost upsets the whole table. "Just a minute. Just a minute please, please!" he pleads. I have seen just exactly his expression in the eyes of a rabbit about to be shot who can't run left, right, or center. The second soldier, on the floor in the parlor, may have died. I can't look at him because I am too afraid.

"India, where are you?" Mama calls.

But I have rushed outside to the street. When my sickness is spent I start to shake. I don't have the strength to go upstairs to my bed, so instead I sit dumbly on the floor near the stairway, hands over my ears.

Through the half-closed kitchen door I can make out Pa lying spread-eagled across the body of the man on the table. Mama has cut the man's trouser leg neatly up the side stripe. The smell of chloroform whooshes out of Doctor Hooks's bottle and catches me in the back of the throat. It takes Junius Hooks thirteen minutes by the clock to saw off the unconscious man's leg just below the knee.

Doctor Hooks brushes past me. He peers under the eye-lids of the boy who has lost his thumb. This time I am asked to hold the chloroformed rag over the boy's mouth and lips. "Hold this arm up steady, India," Dr. Hooks orders me, and I do, not looking. He puts his knee on the boy's chest to hold him down. He threads a surgical needle with his old eyes and trembling fingers. He whips the thread end between his teeth, sharpening it with spit before he gets it through the needle eye right.

Sergeant No-Leg has to be removed upstairs to a bed. Pa and Doctor Hooks make a blanket litter. They put him in my bed.

Mama wire brushes and lye soaps her kitchen table, same as Ester Cooley does after she has prepared a hog for smoking.

In the sudden quiet I try and keep awake but my head bobs in sleep onto my chest. Someone takes the thumbless boy off the stairway. They lay him down on two chairs fac-ing. I only nod awake when Doctor Hooks calls me.

He tells me I must get ahold of myself. We must all be brave like our gallant men.

My eyes brim with frustrated tears. I tell Doctor Hooks I'm doing my best but the sight of blood makes me swimmy-headed. With patience he assures me that I can get the wil-lies out of my system if I pray. "It is the place of a woman to nurse the men in war," he says. He spits into his hands to get some blood off them. He points into the kitchen. "You will be a woman, India, in a year or so. Look at your mama's example! She's a regular surgeon's nurse. Nerves of steel, tower of strength!" says Doctor Hooks.

He bends to examine the soldier stretched out on our floor. "Poor gut-shot boy. He is about to enter the kingdom of heaven. Let him hear a woman's voice in the name of mercy," says Doctor Hooks. "Learn this now, girl. When life is slipping away, the last thing we hear should be the word of the Lord. This man will enter the gates of heaven without a pause in his stride."

Doctor Hooks goes away. I lower myself to the floor beside the collapsed soldier. He has long brown eyelashes that a girl would envy. I guess he is someone's sweetheart, because he is so comely. I reckon he has probably heard the Bible from beginning to end like everyone else. I get out my book from Mr. Reed, *David Copperfield*. I begin on page one and read to him. I reckon that if the last thing he hears is the words of Charles Dickens, it'll be a lot more interesting than Deuteronomy.

Doctor Hooks comes back. He coos to the soldier, easing open the man's shirt and trousers, slipping a hand inside them to see about the wound.

"Our Father," he says, "who art in heaven . . ."

"Mama!" cries the man on the floor.

"Mama is what we all say first and last in the world," Doctor Hooks tells me, and he closes the man's eyes and places two coins upon the lids. We finish the Lord's Prayer.

Does my pa lift me and croon to me? Does he hold me in his arms and tell me I should never have to see such things outside of hell itself? I believe he does, and I only half hear.

———————————————

At sunup the house is clean and airish. Someone has put a blanket over me. Abby is stuffed under it, and I am sure she was not there before. For a still moment I think I have been in a fever and dreamed the whole night, until I notice a rag still tied to the banister like a little flag of war. The two facing chairs are empty.

Pa is home! I tell myself. It is all I care about. I run down to the cellar. There are tins of sugar and coffee in the Yankee knapsacks. I undo their buckles and unload them in the kitchen, lining up their contents along the cupboard. I set out to make flapjacks with molasses and bacon.

Singing softly as I feed wood to the stove, I prepare to tell Pa what has happened since he's left. I want to tell him all about Emory and our world of bottle gardens, crystals, and Colonel Jeb Stuart himself.

I blow the stove fire to life. I want all Pa's stories of the victories, one after another, that the magician Stonewall has won. I want to hear that we'll have licked the Yankees forever by next week.

I make a pot of coffee, measuring it carefully as gold dust, and bring it steaming hot and sugared to Pa and Mama upstairs. My mother is asleep in a chair. Her red eyes blink open.

"Where's Pa?" I whisper.

"Gone back," she says. Mama runs her hand roughly over my cheek and sorts out my tangled hair. "The boy by the stairs," she explains, "he died before dawn. Pa's taken his body back to his mama and papa in Front Royal."

Hope stirs. "But Pa'll be back?"

She plants a woody peck on my shoulder. "Go on along now," she tells me. "Give me that coffee. Dry those tears or there'll be no stopping them."

Sergeant No-Leg is creaking in my bed in the next room. Mama and I hold our breath, wordlessly hoping he'll spare us a few minutes before he wants something or the house fills with screams again.

I drink the coffee I made for Pa. I watch the sky lighten, smelling the coffee steam, the sweat in Mama's dress, and the blood of three men still damp in the folds of her skirt. She pushes my hair out of my eyes and smoothes it back on my head. We do not talk of the events of last night.

THE WAY OF WOMEN

A month after the night of the wounded, I sit in Geneva's front garden watching a thunderstorm gather. I have spent the morning studying Latin with Calvin, who stands in for Emory. Calvin has taught me to use Latin and to write simple poems in it. He has given me a small book to write them in. When Pa comes home I intend to have the book full of short Latin poems and to give it to him. A letter from Pa lies on the grass, weighed down with a stone against the wind.

"What does Cy Moody have to say?" asks Geneva.

"He had to blow up a bridge."

"Where?" she asks. "Why?"

"Across the North Fork of the Shenandoah. He says our army were sitting ducks. Fifteen thousand Southern troops were saved because the bridge was blown up. The Yanks were stopped at the North Fork."

"Well that's a good thing," says Geneva.

"But there's a bad part. That bridge on the North Fork

was the life's pride of my great-grandfather. He built it with his own hands and team. His name was Jobe Sion, and his name was on the bridge. We used to have picnics there next to the river."

"Does your father take it hard?" she asks.

"His writing's blurred with tears in the ink," I say.

The rain comes then. Geneva wants to make sure I don't take a chill. She wants me to help make up a basket for Emory. He has been assigned to Chimborazo Hospital in Richmond. Geneva pulls me against her side under her sheltering arm. We walk to the house. Ringing the hill on which Longmarsh Hall stands are the orchards. They go on so far they are like a country of their own here in our valley. They have just come out of blossom and into early fruit. The smell in the land on a June day must come very close to the smell of heaven.

I stay for a little while in the glass-house laboratory and wait out the rain. I dust the stuffed owl and the minerals. I polish the watch glasses, desiccators, and blowpipes. I keep Emory's plants trimmed and watered. Every day I study my chemistry and my botany. I can only imagine the hospital where he is. It has six thousand patients.

I want his laboratory to be shipshape whenever it is that he can come home for a spell of furlough. Over on the main shelf of the glass house are his precious notebooks. In those books is something alive. It makes me want to get my hands in up to my elbows. Altogether there are 140 notebooks filled with drawings of plants and animalcula, of his experiment results and his observations on science and medicine. I leaf through. Emory has written parts in German. Where is the key to the mystery of fevers? If I knew a hundredth particle of what Emory knows I would use it. But I don't.

On one of Emory's worktables is a lump of stone called cryolite. It is so transparent that it is invisible if you drop it into a beaker of water. Are there mountains somewhere made of this stone, and do they turn clear as ice when it rains? There is so much I do not know and cannot find out.

Geneva comes to the door. "I have shortbread for you," she says. "Ester has just made it." She sits on a folding stool and gives me two of Ester's cookies. "Tell me," says Geneva, "why you look so solemn. Is it your great-grandpa and his bridge?"

"It's Emory being gone," I say.

"Oh, how we miss him," agrees Geneva. Her soft fingers stroke the back of my arm. "Thank the Lord he is not in the regular army. That he is like your father, serving the suffering and not adding to the slaughter."

"I think you must miss Emory the way I miss my pa," I say.

"Yes, I am sure. No more. No less," says Geneva, but she is looking for what is eating at me.

"I miss Emory a different way," I tell her.

"How is that, India?" Geneva asks. She asks it in the quiet way you ask a two-year baby if he's swallowed a penny or not.

"Don't misunderstand! I don't ever, ever want to get married!" I blurt out.

Geneva laughs. She runs her hand down the back of my shoulders and says, "India, one day you'll make a fortunate man a good wife."

"I hate the word *wife*," I say. "Wives are always off to the side." I try and explain and point to the mantel shelf. "There. Wives are like the candlesticks on each side of the big important clock in the middle. Women can never be a middle piece. Always a side piece."

"But that's what God has ordained from the beginning of time, dear India," says Geneva. "It's not so bad after all. Those candlesticks illumine the clock and the whole room with their flames. It's every woman's place to be the light in the life of her family. It is lovely to be that light."

"I want to learn natural philosophy like Emory," I say, "and chemistry. Emory says I have a mind as good as half the young gentlemen he knows at the university who drink brandy fizzes all day and dance with the ladies all night. Emory says I could do it!"

"And dear India, how would you do such a thing? The universities are for men. They do not allow women to matriculate."

"Oberlin College in Ohio accepts women. It has courses in chemistry and biology."

Geneva holds me away from her, smiles, and neatens my

hair. "I believe you," she says. "If any young lady would ever manage it, my determined India would. But you shall be a woman before long. The notion of reading science and medicine will be as charming to you then as dolls in the nursery. You will want to serve a man and have his family because it is in the physical nature of all women to want this. Only madwomen and the religious want anything else."

"Emory believes everything will change forever after the war."

Geneva answers after she thinks for a beat. "Slavery will probably end," she says. "Calvin says so. No matter how slavery is justified, we know in our hearts it is wrong. But no war in the world can change women to men and men to women."

On my way home I see a face peering down from a bank of clouds. The face is bearded and stern with a widow's peak of white hair above the brow. Is Great-grandfather Sion watching from heaven? I remember family picnics, right under the bridge that is a pile of wreckage now. I remember Great-grandfather with his intemperate white hair drawn back in the old-fashioned style. Does he hear Pa's grief at blowing up the bridge? Does he, in heaven, see a new and lighted path for me, his great-grandchild? He does not speak from that great height.

Amos Birdsong

We see Pa again on the first of August 1862. He comes to the door, dust springing off him like a body halo. Under his eyes are bluish yellow pockets.

"Don't touch me, Pussy Willow," he says. "I'm dirty as a dead mule."

Mama takes off his shirt for him. "Might as well throw it out, since you couldn't get a beggar in the sewers of Araby to wear it," she says.

From the backyard I bring in a bucket of water that I've had warming in the sun. Mama begins to wash Pa down. The color drains out of Pa's face. Over he goes in the kitchen chair, arms around his knees.

Mama eases him down on the floor. He lies there, curled up like a dog. After a minute she helps him out to the privy on his elbows and knees because he can't stand up. "Turner Ashby is dead," Pa tells us.

"Ashby and ten alley cats," Mama snaps.

Mama and I wash his hair and tuck him in bed. "He has lost half his body weight," she says. She wants him out of the hell forsaken army.

Pa's eyes flicker up at her when she uses this forbidden word. Mama never swore before the war. But loose language spills out of her every little while now. It goes with the tattered clothing and ragged fingernails.

When Pa is asleep Mama shows me the seams of his trousers. The seam is where the lice hide. She boils the trousers for hours before she's satisfied there's nothing alive in them.

Doctor Hooks comes by after supper with his kit bag of bleeding cups.

"It's the camp fever," says Doctor Hooks. "Every man in the army has it. Comes from the miasmas in the air."

"It comes from contaminated drinking water," I put in.

Doctor Hooks shoots me a half smile and places hot cups on Pa's back. They cause blisters to rise, and then Doctor Hooks bursts the blisters and lets them bleed out. After that he gives Pa castor oil to purge the gut, and a mixture called blue mass to regulate it.

More than half the Confederate Army is sick with the runs that do not cure and go on for months and months. No one knows why. Is this illness kept a secret from the Yanks? If the whole army is this sick how can it fight? "Very carefully," rasps Pa.

Pa has eaten nothing for a month but raw parched corn and bacon fat spread on top of bread all tunneled through by worms. We feed him up on beef tea and sweet yams and snap peas.

I write to Emory in Richmond. "Please, please let me know when new pills come from Germany," I tell him. "My pa has camp fever and needs something better than leeches."

I give Pa boiled water only.

"Why?" asks Mama.

"Because any bacteria in the water are dead after boiling."

"What are these bacteria you are always talking about?" she wants to know.

After a week Pa stops crawling to the privy every ten minutes, but his fever stays, despite Doctor Hooks draining off ill humors in the blood. Finally Pa tells Doctor Hooks to stop. In sleep he yells the word *no! no!* every night. He does not remember this in the day.

While hanging up his tunic I find a silver watch in the pocket. Engraved on its case is *"To our dearest son, Amos Birdsong, from his father and mother."* Who is Amos Birdsong? I open the watchcase and show it to Pa. "Who is Amos Birdsong?"

"Never, never ask me that," he says, and takes the watch.

A week later I cool a bowl of water by blowing on it. I bathe his face. I ask, "Pa?"

"Yes, Pussy Willow."

"Who is Amos Birdsong?"

The canvas awning moves slightly at the window. We watch it together, hoping for a breeze to take up, but it falls back into the heat rising off Buckmarsh Street.

He tells me, "India, when a man goes to war he must oftentimes act more like a woman than a man."

He waits for breath, as if he'd run up a hill. "The boys in my unit are like my sons. I fret when they are sick. I bind up the sores and blisters on their feet when their shoes give out. I feed them the best of my terrible food. I cover them at night when I have no blanket of my own. I am like a mother to my boys. Amos was one of them."

I feel Pa's fingers reach for my hand. Then he is full of sleep.

When he wakes I don't press him on Amos Birdsong. I read him a poem from the Aeneid that I have learned in Latin.

"What does it mean?" asks Pa.

"It means, 'My love for you will never die, although the oceans may try to drown it and the passage of time wear it down, as time wears down the mountains. Love will survive death and everything but forgetting.'"

"Calvin is tutoring you while Emory Trimble is at Chimborazo, isn't he?"

"Yes," I answer.

"You have not been studying your household economics or your Scriptures?" asks Pa.

"I have had enough Scriptures to last three lifetimes."

Pa is content. He does not send me spiky looks through the air like Mama when she catches me at *Elements of Chemistry* and plops the open Bible down on top of my pages.

"I did something you would like to see, Pa. I want to show you next time. When you are well."

"What is that, Pussy Willow?"

"I took a red zinnia out of the Trimbles' garden. Just as my chemistry book says, I held it over a crucible of burning sulfur. The zinnia turned white as snow. It was like a miracle."

"What is a crucible of burning sulfur?" asks Pa.

"Then I dipped the flower in a beaker of water, and the red color was restored. Another miracle!"

"Alchemy!" says Pa.

"Chemistry," says I.

"Do you understand it?" he asks.

"Some of it."

"Tell me why you do this," he says.

"I don't want to live as Mama says I must. Mama has worn a whalebone corset from the time she's been sixteen. All women do. I won't do it."

"It constricts the lungs," agrees Pa. "She's happier when she takes it off."

"It constricts the mind," say I. Then I tell him what is truly in my heart. "Each memorized element, every Latin conjugation, feels like a coin in my pocket. I can use them to pay my way into a world that is out of bounds to any girl, Pa."

Pa shakes his head. "You have the ambition of a boy, not a girl, my little one. You can't get employment as a woman, except maybe as a servant."

"Why does it have to be like that, Pa? I want to study chemistry and biology." I take a shallow and shaky breath. "I want to go to Oberlin College where Julia is, where Alden goes. They take girls at Oberlin."

"My dearest India," says Pa. "I couldn't pay for college if I saved for twenty years. Education's for the rich."

I go to my room where I hide my letters and extract the latest one from Julia. I read it to him. It is all about the college, which seems to be the main draw in the town of Oberlin.

Pa sighs. "We are not the Pardoes."

"I can work to pay my way," I say shakily.

Pa says sadly, "Pussy Willow, we have not a penny to bless ourselves and no way of getting it. The rest of the country laughs at our money. When the war is over everything in the South will be worthless except the land. Without federal dollars you won't even have the train fare to Ohio."

Pa takes my hand and places it over his heart. He hums me a song we sang at bedtime when I was so little and he was so big.

In the evening an officer arrives. He is Captain Davis. Captain Davis rode all the way down to Charlottesville with Pa, driving Turner Ashby's body in his wagon. He wants to tell Pa he has been promoted and given a decoration.

We've put Pa in his dressing gown for this interview with Captain Davis. Pa listens, eyes darting at everything except Captain Davis's face. He cannot understand why he has been honored and promoted.

Captain Davis explains it is because Pa carried Turner Ashby's body off the field. Carried it a mile until he gave it to four horsemen. "He died gloriously" is what Pa is supposed to have said to the four riders.

"I said no such thing!" says Pa. "I didn't even know it was Turner Ashby. I thought it was some cavalry fool who fell off his horse. Why do they put words in my mouth?"

"Oh, yes you did say it, Cy," insists the captain. "Your words were written down on paper by a witness and saved."

"More likely written down in horse manure," grumbles Pa.

Turner Ashby, life, death, and last words sounds to me like a story out of mythology.

Pa looks at his promotion, drops it to the floor, and doubles over with cramp. He stumbles back outside to the privy.

Captain Davis leans forward to Mama. He whispers to her that the army needs Pa back. "He is the best man in Northern Virginia with horses," says Captain Davis. "No man drives an ambulance wagon with such skill. No man is more important in General Jackson's quartermaster's corps than Cyrus Moody," Davis tells her. "I know you'll get him well right soon, Mrs. Moody."

Mama nods her head. She doesn't argue with men. What's the good?

"Sometimes he falls asleep in the privy," she says. "I better get him."

Captain Davis turns to me pleasantly. His face is well scrubbed and honest. Unlike Ma I look him in the eye. I ask him who is Amos Birdsong.

"A deserter," says Captain Davis. "'Birdsong was a cheap, devious little deserter, and he got what was coming to him." I hear the story Pa will not tell me.

Mama has no time for any more fancy officers. She's got Pa in bed again and sends me off to fetch Doctor Hooks.

Doctor Hooks comes by to place hot bricks covered in flannel on Pa's stomach. He says they will draw out the impurities in the blood and break the fever. By the time I finish with Eddie and Grandpa Moody and get upstairs, the doctor has gone and Pa's heart has begun to beat very fast. It's hot as a bread oven in Pa's bedroom. He begs me to remove the hot bricks from his stomach. I put cool water in a basin so he can put his feet in. I put a cool cloth on the back of his neck until his pulse stops racing.

"Captain Davis told me about Amos Birdsong," I say.

Pa whispers, "What did Davis tell you?"

"He said Amos Birdsong was a slacker and a deserter and had a fair-square court-martial and was sentenced to death by firing squad. That you were selected by lots to command his execution. That you were a brave man and Amos was a coward and General Jackson had to deal with cowards so they didn't rot the whole barrel of apples."

Pa gets back into bed. I fan him with a newspaper.

Pa says, "Amos Birdsong only tried to get home a few days to help his mama put in their corn seed. He'd had no leave or furlough in a whole year. He couldn't even write home because he'd never learned. He was seventeen years and three days old."

Pa sips some water and finishes. "They made him sit in his own coffin on the way to his execution. He screamed like an animal, India. That's the only kind of scream I've heard like this. I untied his handcuffs. Let him sit next to me and rocked him like a baby. I put my hat on him because they shaved his head and it was burning in the sun. His tears soaked the front of my shirt like sweat. He wanted to go home and help his mama is all!"

"Pa, did you have to shoot Amos Birdsong?"

"I went to the captain. Captain, I say, I drive ambulances. I don't shoot young boys. Look at this soldier's face. He doesn't even shave yet. How can you shoot him? He might be your little brother!"

I squeeze a rag of water over Pa's forehead to get it back from fiery red.

He goes on, "The command to fire came. I fired over the boy's head into the trees. So did the whole squad. The commander's bullet hit him in the heart. His best friend and I buried Amos on a hill where the wind blew over. I had no marker or time to carve one. So I wrote his name out in pebbles. I pressed them into the earth over where he lay."

Angel of Death

Going into September 1862, Mama keeps her eye out the window. "I get my man back, get him well, and that sloe-eyed Captain Davis will turn up like a bad penny," Mama says.

On September tenth Pa takes me out shooting to see if we can get a buck for the winter. He stumbles like an old man next to me. I carry his gun.

"I'm going to teach you to shoot, India," he says. "Might as well. You're doing all that boy-learning so you might as well be a crack shot and learn to ride and drive a wagon like a boy, too. Who knows what this world will bring your way?" Pa says this as if he might not be there to see it, and a little chill goes through me.

All day companies of soldiers pass, heading north. Going up to Harpers Ferry, they say to us, maybe to western Virginia. The soldiers seem to be pulled by an invisible force, like wild geese on their way north. Our Confederate Army is so pitiful, so thirsty and hungry. Some men are feeble as scarecrows, hair uncut, shoeless. Their filthy trousers wave in the breeze.

I am mindful of the way things were just before Julia left. Our boys in gray went off to battle clean as whistles, cheeks full of pretty girls' kisses. Now it is different.

I watch them and wave a little, shyly.

"Hey, purty little girl!" some say. "Say hi to my mama!"

Where are their mamas? A hundred miles away? I bite my lip, thinking of the healthy Yanks in their neat blues.

"This is General Lee's Army of Northern Virginia," says Pa. "Isn't it just a sight! But don't let 'em fool you. Each one can take on four Yanks." Pa is looking for his regiment, but he doesn't find it.

"Pa, you're not well enough to do more than sit at table," I tell him. "We've just walked a little way today and you can't carry your gun and you're out of breath, ready to go home."

A lieutenant passes us and claps the flat of his saber against his horse's side. "Move up!" he yells at nobody we can see. "Move on up!"

Pa knows that a big battle is cooking. One of the men has lost his company, a farmer from Hamilton County. He comes along home with Pa and me for something to eat.

Mama gives our visitor a slice of fatback and pickled melon rinds, then some of her precious Yankee coffee. The sergeant takes off his hat and begs her pardon for the way he smells. He goes out and splits a half a cord of wood for us. This he stacks against the house. Mama washes his shirt and tunic for him while he takes a lick-and-a-promise bath at the pump.

I hand him a good willow twig to brush his teeth. "Oh, little miss, git yourself out of here," he whispers. "Git out of northern Virginia! Ain't you got no relatives no place else?" He splashes cold water into his armpits.

Always I watch Pa carefully. He sleeps restlessly, brow covered with sweat. Is he getting ready to leave us soon? Somewhere on a ship, on a train, is a small package of silver-colored pills from Germany. Every night when I say my prayers I pray one thing. That package will come from Emory so that I can get the medicine into Pa and maybe stop his fevers.

In front of our house we hand out water by the dipperful to the river of men going north on Buckmarsh Street, until our rain barrel is empty.

Pa lies in bed for hours, but he does not sleep.

Captain Davis comes to our house the evening of the sixteenth of September.

"I knew we'd see your face again," says Mama.

The captain is all smiles and cold as charity. "Cy Moody will not be in the path of danger," he says to Mama. "He will not even need to walk. But we sorely need him, ma'am, to drive our ambulance wagons."

"What is going to happen?" I ask. "Where are all the troops heading?"

"Maryland," says Captain Davis. "General Lee is going to tuck it to the Yanks. After tomorrow the Yanks will surrender, Lincoln will resign, and the war will be over."

"My boys will be asking for me," says Pa. He struggles to his feet, then sinks back into his chair.

"Captain Davis!" Mama grabs the captain, but it is no good. She tells him Pa has a fever that soaks the bed all night. It does no good.

Captain Davis pats Mama's hand. "I have quinine in the wagon," he says. "He'll be right as rain with a dose of quinine."

Doctor Hooks has given Pa quinine for the last six weeks. It does as much good as a puff of smoke.

Davis helps Pa into his uniform and then to the door. The captain opens it and waits with one hand on Pa's sleeve. I see my father turn, crinkle a smile at us, and leave in the evening light. I see the light catch his hair.

Mama and I keep our eyes on the spot in the parlor where we say good-bye.

"That little spot is all we've got," says Mama. "The air just rushes into the space he left."

A chill runs down my back. Some law of probability tells me that Pa has been like a cat with nine lives who has just lived through life number eight. I square up my shoulders and hold my breath against crying, hold my feet against running out the door and up the street after Pa. I want to hobble Captain Davis's horse and get Pa back here for one more night. I know I have to take care of Mama. Mama and Eddie and Grandpa. *You have to be the strong one, India!* says a voice in my head, and I choke off my tears in my throat. It is Pa's voice that speaks.

Mama won't eat. Late that night she comes in and sits on the side of my bed.

I ask her, "Did I cry out? Did I wake you?"

She shakes her head no.

"What is it, Mama? Your hands are like ice."

"Where is he?" she asks.

"Mama, Captain Davis will take care of him."

"Where is my Cy?" she asks.

"Mama, Pa's all right. He's just driving the ambulance. He doesn't go near the battle. Captain Davis said how valuable he is. They'll take care of him. One more battle and he'll come on home and the war will be over." Do I believe my own words?

"India," she whispers. "I believe I saw an angel. It scared me to death."

"An angel?" I ask. "With wings and everything?"

"It came through the window of my bedroom. The wing brushed up on my face."

"Oh, Mama, it was a dream is all," I say. "Just a dream."

She shakes her head. "Look how bright the full moon is," she says. "I saw it come in the room with my own eyes, clear as day. Here, look! Where the wing touched my cheek, it left a little trace."

"I can't see anything on your cheek, Mama. There's nothing there." I hold Mama across the shoulders. She is so thin because she can't eat from worrying.

"If anything happens to your pa we will lose his salary— such as it is. We might become refugees on the road," she says. "You see them all the time. Families who've lost their men."

"We're not going to be refugees, Mama," I say. "And nothing bad will happen to Pa."

Just before dawn I hear a dog bark. I open the front door. On our steps is a small parcel. It has a freight label from the Richmond train. Emory has sent me something. I tear open the paper. His note reads,

"I hope your pa is better now, India. I have these pills from another visiting doctor from Heidelberg University in Germany. They are Salicin, the same as were given to my brother Tommy at Christmas, and might have saved Tommy's life if he had paid attention and taken the full dose. The pills are made of Weidnerinde, or ground willow bark. They stop fevers and headaches and all manner of other pain.

Give them once in evening and once in morning.

I have seen them cure men of camp fever here in the hospital. Your father should recover in about a week if he takes them faithfully.

Your great friend, Emory Trimble

In the tin box are a score of tiny pills like steel dots. I close the box and rattle them. I will follow Captain Davis and find my pa if it's the last thing I do.

What War Is

I stuff the box of ampules in the bodice of Abby's dress and let myself into the Spreckles' pasture to borrow their mare, Lorena. I put on her bridle and jump on her wide bare back. She knows me, and she carries me comfortably.

The countryside north to Charles Town is empty of soldiers now, but their trail is easy enough to follow. Gray powder covers every leaf and blade of grass. There are no latrines for twenty thousand men with chronic diarrhea just like my pa. People used to be modest about this. They used to be embarrassed, but no more. It is just another part of constantly being directly inside of the war. I breathe through my mouth and keep my eyes on the hills.

In the late morning we cross into western Virginia and stop at Charles Town. There is a growling in the air of the Maryland hills ahead. A frightening cloud of red dust looms in the sky. I follow that up, eating from a sack of pears. Not a living soul in Shepherdstown shows their face in the streets. A big woman in a tartan plaid dress peeks out a basement window. She bounds up the cellar stairs and insists I shelter with her family. "Don't go any farther," warns a man's voice from below. "You can hear with your very own ears there's more'n twenty thousand guns up there. Canister, grape, musket, and cannons all going off like the Fourth of July."

In another house a preacher and his wife tell me they think the battle is five miles north, near the town of Sharpsburg, where the Antietam Creek runs through. "Come in for some tea, child, till it's over, for pity's sake," they beg me.

But I won't stay in Shepherdstown or shelter with strangers. "I want to find my pa!" I explain to them. "I have medicine for him. He will die of fever without it."

The sun has spent the worst of the day's heat by the time Lorena and I come near Sharpsburg, but there is no entering the town. The battle cloud is now iron brown and hangs like a curtain in the sky. Shells explode all over the place, blowing up huge patches of earth and pit-holing the roads. We ride up to the highest place we can find before Lorena stops and will not go any farther. She points her ears backward and dances sideways back and forth. I hop off and try to settle her, but she yanks her head and reins from me. I wipe flecks of foam from her mouth and tie her in the shade of the biggest tree I can find. Then I breathe into her nostrils and talk to her until she snorts and relaxes. Pa made her bridle, I recall. His initials *CM* are engraved on the brass temple plate. I run my fingers twice down the slickness of the reins.

Abby in my arms, I pick my way up along a deer track, through brambles and groves of pin oak. Suddenly I come out in the open to a knot of civilian strangers in folding chairs. They form a circle with a view of the surrounding countryside. They have field glasses and picnic baskets like the picnickers at our Clarke County races.

One family offer sandwiches. I accept hungrily.

Around us the pounding artillery blocks the sound of what people say. Instead we must all read lips and talk with hand motions. On the actual battlefield below us the great mortars and Napoleon cannons boom, shooting their screaming shells, loud as direct-overhead thunderstorms. From deep in the innards of the earth where I stand eating a hard-boiled egg, come echoing rumbles. At each new fusillade the ground under my feet shudders and bucks with exploding rage.

A gentleman in a checkered city suit invites me to look out over the battle through his spyglass. He shouts in my ear that he is a reporter for a Baltimore newspaper.

He places his spyglass against my eye. I don't know what I am seeing or where to look.

"Over there," he says. "This morning at ten o'clock that was a cornfield."

There is no cornfield. There is earth in strange lumps,

thousands of mouse-colored mounds. Some seem to move. I ask what they are.

He tells me. "Those are bodies. Most probably dead by now. Some alive. No one can help the wounded ones until the sun sets and both sides stop shooting."

I step back, as if the eyepiece were red-hot.

The reporter says, "I don't know what to write about this. All day I've been counting troops. You can count a company, a battalion, a regiment, pretty easy if you know how an army is set up. I reckon there's ten, fifteen, twenty thousand men lying on the ground here. Most in that cornfield. This morning at nine o'clock there were thirty acres of sweet field corn ready to harvest. An hour later every stalk of corn in the field was individually brought down by a bullet. You couldn't cut that field down so neat if you had a dozen field hands with scythes."

On the next rise from us a line of men in blue coats face a straight row opposite of men in gray. They are actually formed up like boys in a schoolyard game. The rifles appear to be sticks. Then they all shoot at once, and both sides fall down on their backs dead. We cannot hear the guns over the roar.

Far away an officer in a red shirt wheels his horse and directs his division against a regiment of Yanks. His troops mow them all down. They tumble like pushed-over toys.

"See that creek there?" says the reporter. "That's Antietam Creek. This afternoon the stream itself ran blood not water." He adds, "That officer in the red shirt is probably General Hill. He's got fresh troops. You can see the battle fever is on him."

"What is battle fever?"

"Well it's like a delirium," he explains. "Battle fever comes over a man when he's in the thick of a fight and sees his way to killing a hundred men. They say it's like a kick of opium. He fills up on oxygen. People say a good general in the heat of battle gets his blood running so fast his heart expands up to the size of a horse's heart. Some of them, like Stonewall, can go without breathing for four or five minutes. It's all the death they cause, you see? It makes a commander feel like God. Right this very minute I'd bet a ten-spot General Hill's eyes can see five miles."

"Why don't they stop?" I ask. "Haven't they killed enough?"

My reporter man shakes his head. "Women don't understand it, but that's what war is."

The last artillery shell bursts and the guns peter out in the coming evening. Then it is too dark for field glasses or a spyglass. The moon comes out low over the town of Sharpsburg. Like the Antietam Creek running blood, the moon is a brooding red.

"Look! Look at the moon!" the reporter says. The moon is in its last quarter. It appears low on the horizon above the smoke. The crescent sits like a bloody smile in the sky. I hide my eyes from it and slip away as if I lived nearby.

The deer track that I easily followed this afternoon has disappeared in the dark woods. Suddenly I hear the swish of a woman's skirt ahead of me.

"Mama!" I cry out. It can't be my mama but it looks something like her. The woman does not turn at my voice. "Mama!" I cry again, and run my forehead smack into a pine branch. My daytime high spirit skivvies out of me like a pitcher of water poured out on the ground. I cry with the pain and hold Abby against myself.

"Hold on, girl, hold on," I tell myself. I dig my nails into the palms of my hands to stop panic welling up. I try to concentrate on the sound of the skirt. I try to see through the mist that spirals up from the earth. But this isn't a usual evening mist. It is something else. It rises off hundreds of dead and dying soldiers.

My calling voice carries only an inch beyond my lips, then fails. Everywhere I step lies a soldier. I must leap over them. "Mama, don't leave me behind!" I yell, but the woman is only a shadow in the trees down the hill.

Frozen where they fell down lie uncountable numbers of men. I look at their faces for just half a second and think they might as well be the fathers of my friends. Then I must turn away mortified, because some of them have ripped their clothes off as they died. I have no water or comfort to give anyone who is still slightly moving.

Twilight deepens to night. Only a little white church glows somewhere in the darkness. I cannot go backward or forward because I can't see where I am stepping.

All at once on the hillside opposite, a galaxy of lanterns blinks to life. On the hilltops the wicks are lit, one, and another, and another. They are the field hospital lights. Pa has two such in his ambulance wagon. Pa is among them, somewhere.

The medics form a new army descending on the dying like a regiment of fireflies. Then the lamps drift soundlessly out to the pastures already piled with the dead. They are separating the savable.

The lamps are on the ground or held aloft while the medics cast around, bending and turning in circles.

A lamp is wavering down the hill toward me. It swings up on me, and suddenly two big country hands steady me.

"What in the name of Jesus is a kid like you doing here? A girl! A little filly in a plaid dress with a doll in her hand?" His voice is pure Tennessee. He is an infantryman, big as two men and straw haired.

"I'm trying to find my pa," I answer.

"Well, welcome to it. One half the army's out looking for the other half. You leave now!" he orders. "I will show you the way. When we get the wounded boys off the field, the whole damned Rebel army will head back to Virginia before the boys in blue kill the other half of them. Little sister, this here is a church supper compared to tomorrow. And the next day'll be worse than that."

"How could anything be worse?"

"Poor simple little girl," he says. "Go home. This ain't no place for a nice girl."

"I can't go. I have to find my pa," I try to tell him. "My pa has the camp fever. If he doesn't get his medicine he will die."

Tennessee's face and voice rise up impatient and twangy. "Listen good, sister," he says. "Tomorrow thousands of dead men will turn black and bloat like sausage in the sun. Their trousers can't contain their guts. You don't wanna see that ever in your lifetime."

"No," I agree suddenly.

"It takes months to clean up a battlefield. The lowest orderlies get a quart of rum down 'em and they bury the dead 'cause only a drunk can stand the smell. This is all pure fact, girl. I only tell you so you leave good and quick."

The strength quits out of me. He is sorry and supports me as I settle on the ground. "That's what war is, girl. That's what war is!"

He squats next to me and gives me a little water. "Look up. Look at that sickle moon! It's as red as blood. I never did imagine anything as bad as this could ever be on the face of the earth. I can hardly breathe," he says sadly.

I nod and wipe my eyes and nose on my sleeve.

"What's your doll's name?"

"Abby," I answer.

"I got a sister with a doll, too," he says.

We sit in the circle of light cast by his friendly lantern. I get up to brush off my skirt.

"Wait, now before you go," says Tennessee. "Little missy, you're here and you might as well stay just a tick. You will see the peculiarist thing in the world, like the actual face of the Lord. It happens every time, but the men never talk about it. Watch now," he tells me suddenly. "Blink and you'll miss it."

In front of us a soldier is crumpled in a heap, his legs draped over a log. His arms are raised above his head, stiff as iron pokers.

"Look at the breast of that man's tunic, now. Look, look!" Tennessee holds my hand in his and points.

A little teaspoon of light, green as a cat's eye, winks out from the soldier's breast. It pops from between two buttons and holds still three inches over the top of him. Whatever it might be, it's as slight as a baby's sigh.

"What is that?" I pull back from it.

"Look careful now!" urges my friend, and he takes my elbow like I'm bound to faint.

For one beat of a heart, the thirty-acre cornfield is a carpet of emerald stars. No bigger than dollar pieces, they spill from the fallen men as far as a person can see. Then they bubble upward and vanish into the blackness of the sky.

My Tennessee friend steers me to an uphill path and gives me his lantern. "Some people say it's swampfire," he whispers, "but it was the souls going up."

My Inland Sea

Tennessee places me in a soft bed of grass, with no brambles or bodies nearby, and tucks his army blanket over me.

"Sleep," he whispers. "Sleep, little girl. Then run like hell out of here when daylight comes."

I know nothing more until someone plucks at my shoulder. She has kindly eyes, this lady, all pretty in her embroidered red vest. She pours something from a kettle into a cup for me. It is soup, good and hot with pepper in it.

The red moon of the night before is gone. The cheerful sun has no idea what it shines down upon. The lady in the vest kneels on the grass beside me and counts money into a cloth bag. A stumpy, black-haired man also in an embroidered vest joins her and says something I cannot understand. He puts down a very heavy bag. Out of it come billfolds. He riffles through them, empties them of their letters and photographs. These he tosses away. He keeps the money, jewelry, rings, and pocket watches in another pile. His wife has a small campfire going. She gives him a cup of soup and offers another one to me.

He smiles nearly toothlessly at me. "Yankee only. Rebel boys have no money. No jewelry. I go only to Yankee bodies." With his teacup hand he points to the acres of dead soldiers that lie on the hillsides. "Gold rings!" he says. "Officers are best. Why bury the jewelry in the grave? Tell me why? So I take them."

They are not alone. Carefully stepping from fallen soldier to fallen soldier, an army of scavengers stoops all over the battlefield. They unbutton tunics, take what is in the breast pocket, scatter the debris they cannot use, and go on to the next.

The gypsies offer me black bread spread with butter, which I eat hungrily. Then I get up and say good-bye. I find my pin oak tree fifty yards uphill.

Lorena whinnies at me. She is cropping grass contentedly, as if there'd been no shot fired for a hundred miles.

I untether her and find water for her in a branch of the big Antietam Creek. The stream runs clear as glass. While she drinks I wash my hands and face. Then, over on the opposite side of the sloping bank, I see him. A man in a blue uniform is comfortably curled on a bed of moss under an umbrella of silver cloak fern. I hold my breath so as not to wake him.

There is a small hole in his temple. The wound looks too small to really count for much, but he is dead, surely enough. I unbutton his beautiful blue tunic and for just a second slip my hand inside to the wallet, which sits untouched and still warm. It is so easy to do this.

Lorena and I join up to the Berryville Pike heading south until the sun is low in the Virginia sky. It is the only way I will find Pa now. He is no doubt driving one of the ambulances in a ribbon of endless wagons. The traffic is going my way. As far as I can see back to Sharpsburg and on to Berryville, the road is congested with ambulance wagons. The cries from inside the canvas covers might as well come from the underworld itself. I have seen these men last night lying on hillsides, some with their faces blown clear off their heads.

I ask after Pa among the drivers, but no one has seen him. Somebody tells me, "Robert E. Lee's army is half-killed, half–run off. Don't know about the Yanks."

I reach the Spreckles' house, head down. I expect to get an earful from Mama for running off without telling anyone where I was going. But the Spreckles tell me Mama left the morning I did. She walked all the way to Sharpsburg to find Pa and bring him home. Grandpa Moody and Eddie are safe with the Spreckle sisters. The sisters haul out their big zinc bathtub the moment they lay eyes on me. They fill it with kettle after kettle of warm water and put me in it with a bar of laundry soap. When I am clean and dry they give me corn bread and acorn coffee. "Mama will come soon," they tell me four or five times.

The sisters do not mind the work of Eddie and Grandpa Moody. They let Eddie scramble all over and laugh at everything he does. They cut up Grandpa Moody's dinner just right so he can eat it all by himself.

I hear nothing all day and the next but our beaten army creaking past. Some are just old buck wagons with the torn-to-pieces men roasting in the sun. There are no latrines for them, no water or shade or food or medicine.

"Do you know Sergeant Cy Moody?" I ask each of the ambulance drivers. No one knows where he is.

We take in some of the exhausted men and give them water and biscuits. In this way the Spreckle sisters' kitchen becomes a living newspaper of nonsense and fact. It's impossible to know which is which. We learn that twenty thousand men fell, both sides, in the cornfield and on a road called Bloody Lane. Our army has lost nearly a half, but the other half escaped the Union without being chased. So the entire horrible battle winds up neither a victory nor a defeat for either side.

On the evening of the third day after the battle, someone brings Mama back to us. Her dress is stained with blood, six inches up from the hem, from walking the battlefield. Mama's eyes are as lifeless as coins.

Maybelle, Pa's horse, is now blinded and comes back with

Mama. Maybelle's eyes got all blued over, in an accident. That is what Mama tells us, and that's all. She actually tells it to the ceiling. Pa is missing. He is absolutely not dead, only missing.

Mama looks right at me but doesn't see me. It is so frightening I open my mouth to try and breathe, but there is no available air in the room.

"India, Cy Moody can't be found just now," she says. "Don't let anyone tell you different. He is busy, busy, busy with the wounded. He will come home when he's finished."

In the evening, while Mama is asleep, Captain Davis appears at the door. He asks to see my mother. The Spreckles will not let him. Neither will I.

"She is in a state, Captain," they tell him. "Leave her be, the poor woman."

I ask, "What do you want, Captain Davis?" but I know what he wants. He wants to judge if I am going to scream or take this news quietly. Finally he can't avoid just telling it out.

"Cy Moody passed away in a field hospital, the day after the battle," he explains gently. "He ran a fever and his heart gave out."

"Oh," is all I can answer, before the fast beating of my own heart stops all words.

"He didn't sleep for thirty hours straight, working with the wounded." Davis looks up and wipes across his mouth with his sleeve, as if this can make the words come out different. "We buried him on the north side of the church with the rest of our dead."

"Oh," I answer again, tongue thick in my mouth.

"I am so sorry, Miss Moody. He was a brave man and a good soldier."

"My mama is not ready to hear it just yet," is all I can say. I have expected this. I knew this all along. I tell myself at least Pa was not shot. The memory of the red moon night surges back at me, bringing me the images I have been trying to push out of my mind for three days. My mind says quickly, *At least Pa was not lying for hours without water, undoing his trouser buttons, screaming against the pain, the sun, the flies. At least his face has not been blown away like some of them. At least he was not lying in a muddy ditch with no legs and no hands. At least that.* I am dizzy and sit down on the floor.

Grace Spreckle lays her hands on my shoulders. Captain Davis digs in his pocket. He produces five brass buttons. "I cut these off his tunic," he says. "I thought you'd like to have them." He produces a rumpled piece of paper with scratch lines penciled in. "This here's a diagram, a little map of where we laid him. Right to the north side of the church maybe six feet from the wall. There's a maple tree over him if you ever . . . decide to . . ." His thought peters out. He salutes me. The muscle in Captain Davis's jaw trembles out of control. I hate Captain Davis more than any living person. At the same time I know he has done the best he can.

The buttons sit in my hand after Captain Davis leaves. Mama sewed these very buttons onto Pa's uniform the day before we last saw him.

Grace Spreckle makes me tea and puts a little whiskey in it. The smell of the whiskey nauseates me and I go to the doorway to calm my fluttering stomach. I press my face deeply into some honeysuckle to smell that innocent sweetness instead. I know I have to be quiet in front of Mama.

"I am going out," I say to Grace.

"Where to, child? You look like a ghost. Stay!"

"I am going in to Berryville to sleep in my own bed," I answer.

Grace Spreckle stands in the doorway not knowing what to say. My breath comes in short bursts. My hands shake as I place the bit at the back of Lorena's mouth and fix her girth snugly. Grace asks me to bring back a clean dress for my mama. The dress Mama is wearing will ever remind her and me of the Sharpsburg fields and the men bleeding like freshets in the ground for miles around.

It is three miles to Berryville. In our house is everything of Pa's, his shirts, his boiled clean trousers, his long oiled leather straps placed so neatly over the wooden bars against the parlor wall where he worked at night. It is almost as if he is here again. As if I can have one last good-bye because he is still so fresh in the room. Only four days ago did Pa leave with Captain Davis. Pa has not yet receded into last week or month, as he will all too soon.

I sit in Pa's customary chair and bury my face in his shirt where his smell still lives. I am aware of a sudden force, as if I have been flung through space at the speed of a comet. I know what this speeding ahead is without being told. It is me being hurled forward in time to the empty spot at the head of my family. It is a place where I was not meant to be for years to come, and now I'm there.

I sleep with Pa's unfinished reins, his unstitched harness leathers, and all his clothing in my bed, covering me. I think of how far the star on which he now resides can be from me, back here on earth. My heart screams profanities at the war.

———◆———

The Spreckle sisters do every little thing they can for Mama. They bring in Doctor Hooks. He gives Mama morphine called laudanum. It puts her to sleep. "She knows he is gone but won't say so," explains Doctor Hooks. "Grief is like milk fever. It lingers and nothing helps it but time."

Doctor Hooks takes supper with the sisters and me. He brings the Winchester paper. Its headlines reveal in big black type that President Lincoln has put forth a proclamation freeing all the slaves in the Southern states. "We will now lose the war," says Junius Hooks.

"Well, won't the war end if slavery's ended?" I ask.

"It is too late for the war to end," says Doctor Hooks. "Both sides are too angry."

The laudanum wears off. Mama keeps a handkerchief over her face. She says Pa is calling her from the front yard. She can hear him at all hours and she can smell the battlefield at every moment.

Doctor Hooks gives her oil of cloves to block the smell. "The smell is all in her head," he says. "India, your pa is gone, poor girl, but your mama is addled by his death. Seek comfort in the Lord, because He is testing your character."

How I am to seek that comfort Doctor Hooks does not prescribe.

"Do not tell your ma what you know about your pa. Him being buried behind the Sharpsburg church and all. Don't tell her that. She's not a bit ready," the Spreckles instruct me when they decide it is time for us to go back home to our house. "She is so weak now that she can't take the truth. She must begin to eat again and sleep again before she is told. That is the way it is done."

"Not tell?" Pa's death sits so heavily in me that I am sure the world can see my grief like a rock sticking out of my heart.

The Spreckles shake their heads in unison. "She's not ready. She'll likely break apart. Let her work like normal. Remember, India, if your mama breaks up you can't do by your ownself for your grandpappy and little Eddie. If your mama falls apart we'll have to get word to those biggity relatives you hate over to Kettletown to take on your family."

I calculate this possibility. "I won't say Pa's dead. I won't say anything."

"Let her believe he's coming home. Just like before," say the sisters.

And I do. In the middle of feeding Eddie or Grandpa, in the middle of cleaning the floor, Mama's attention wanders always to the window light in the front door.

"I thought it might be your pa," she says, "just coming home."

"No, Ma," I say. "It wasn't him. It was someone else passed by. He'll come soon. You wait."

"He's down back to Chancellorsville picking up the dead and wounded," she says. "There's so many of 'em for him to tend he can't get a furlough."

I half believe her sometimes. Sleep comes to me unsurely, and I wake in a panic to voices I am sure are in my room. A certain dream comes over and over again. I dread it but cannot wake from it, and so learn to dread even sleep.

It always begins with the reporter's spyglass. Its eyepiece is already at my eye, my full tin of pills safely in hand. I can barely see the small white church in the valley. I have but a minute to run there before Pa dies. I throw away the spyglass but run so slowly that when I get to the church there is no one but a boy without a thumb.

It is Geneva whose words ease me. She tells me I must give myself a time each day to think of nothing and no one but Pa. To keep Pa in the front of my mind during that remembering time. To talk to him. "Although you cannot hear him answer, he surely hears you," says Geneva. "There is only one small silver lining to grief. That is knowing we shall see the ones we love again in heaven. They are gone only for the rest of our lives down here, and then we shall see them again."

Winter comes in early in 1862, as if it wants to make all of life one big November. In the still darkness of Emory's glass house I light the oil lamp and take out my materials. By dropping calcium in a beaker of liquid ammonia I create a tiny ocean of startling blue.

Emory has told me this particular blue is the color of the water along the beaches of Cuba, which he has seen in his travels. I hold the beaker against the brightness of the lamp. The blue against the light washes away the stain of the terrible battlefield, the headless, the voiceless tangle of men, matching the color of the earth, soon to join that earth.

On the white beach of an imaginary Cuba I sit beside my own inland sea and try to heal my mind.

The Chemistry
of Common Life

"The Latin language is like a small and elegant country," says Calvin. "You must learn its turning roads, but once you do you will travel there with ease. Hide your grief in Latin's landscapes, India."

Geneva leads me to the piano and begins me on scales. She shows me her watercolor set and teaches me the rudiments of drawing. "In these arts," says Geneva, "you will find beauty, India, and in beauty is the only escape from pain and memory."

But it is with chemistry that I fill my waking hours. Emory has sent a new book to me. It is Griffin's *Chemical Recreations.* Calvin loves it right along with me. We turn lead salts black with hydrogen sulfide. We experiment with cobalt salts and silver salts.

Mama catches me studying Griffin's as I lie in bed. The candle, which is a rare thing to find in the war, draws her to my door.

"Where's that candle from, India?" she asks me, and pulls her woolen bed jacket around her shoulders because she is always cold.

"Ester Cooley gave it to me up in the Longmarsh kitchen," I tell her.

"I hope you are reading the Scriptures by its light."

"No, Mama."

"What is that book, India? Let me see it."

I hide it under my coverlet. "It is called Griffin's *Chemical Recreations*," I say.

She sits down heavily on the end of my bed.

"Why, India? Why?" she asks.

"Just because. I want to learn."

"Why do you wish to learn men's science, India?"

"Because I do. Because I love it. It is like . . . firelight to me, Mama."

She makes a disgusted sound with her tongue and looks away. "I will have to speak to Calvin and Geneva."

"Mama, please! We have enough trouble without worrying about what I read."

"What do you mean, India, enough trouble? What do you mean by that?"

"Nothing, Mama."

"This is making you godless, India. Someday you'll be a spinster fit for no man. That is what you will become, because no man will have a wife who gets above herself."

She leaves the room sobbing, and I sit alert. Could this be the beginning of her breaking down?

But she goes quiet. Only Eddie cries in his bed. I go sit with him. "Papa," says Eddie. "Papa coming!"

"Soon, Eddie. Soon soon. Shhh now," I say, but cannot bear my own words.

———————————◆———————————

Underneath all this book learning Calvin knows how the world turns. "Women have as much chance of work in the sciences as ice-skating up the river Styx," says Calvin. But we keep on. "Perhaps," says Calvin, "there will be a different world after the war."

It is late June 1863 when Emory comes back on furlough from the Richmond hospital. On that day I am busy labeling all the rocks in his rock collection with new readable labels instead of his hasty scrawl. Suddenly Emory creeps up and stands behind me until I turn in surprise.

"Forgive me for startling you! I had to see what expression was on your face!" he says, smiling.

"Why?" I ask.

"I wished to see how welcome I was, without you having time to pretend!"

"I have been thinking of no one but you!" I blurt out. "Look! I have organized everything in the laboratory, specimens, rocks, even Buddha is dusted and his feathers put right!"

Emory takes me by both hands and we stand together among the ferns. "I am so pleased to see you!" is all he needs to say.

The ferns and the date palm are healthy and bright green against the whitewashed glass panes. We have no words, but smile into each other's eyes. A Bible School lesson rings in my ear—"Have not lewd thoughts nor turn ye to the comeliest of men."

"You are taller!" he says, stepping back, nearly overturning a cactus pot.

"Older!" I say.

"You are fifteen now?" he asks.

"Fourteen and a half."

"I have a new book for us." He pulls it from his satchel. It is called *The Chemistry of Common Life.*

Emory and I consume an entire week with *The Chemistry of Common Life.* We create fountains of fire with phosphorous. Emory pours sulfuric acid into a sugar bowl, raising a pillar of carbon.

On the last morning of his leave he pulls out a huge notebook.

"Can you read my handwriting?" he asks.

"Most of the time," I answer. "You write like a spider. Your *W*s look like teepees!"

"Here, in this book, are my notes from my patients at the hospital," he explains. "Will you transcribe them for me?

Will you organize these notes so that they make sense for me to write a publishable paper?"

My pulse kicks up just a little. I cannot wait to do this. I feel my eyes light. I can't stop them. "What is the paper to be?" I ask.

"In November our hospital invited a visitor from Edinburgh in Scotland. He's a young doctor who works with the finest surgeons there. This Scottish doctor told us a professor of surgery there is trying to solve the mystery of infection in the operating room. I told him I had already solved it. My patients live because I sterilize my instruments."

My eyes do not leave Emory's.

"So the Scottish fellow says to me, 'And have you shown them this in the hospital?'

"'Of course!' I say, 'Everybody knows. I use alcohol. It kills every germ on my scalpel. The other doctors think I'm crazy. They don't believe me. Their ideas are preserved in amber from medieval times.'"

"What did he say to that?"

"Oh, in his Lowlands brogue he says to me, 'Wait and see, young man, our Doctor Lister will be the first to prove this theory, and his name and Scotland's will live in history, because we will publish it at the University of Edinburgh. You Americans are in the middle of a bloody war. You'll never catch up.'"

Then Emory smiles a little sadly. "It's so hard to do this

in America. Every doctor must have these facts. Every doctor! How can they be reached and convinced? That's the question. It isn't a matter of proving this is true. It's a huge mountain to get important doctors to believe it and change. I would like to lead this charge. Even if I am a Rebel boy." He grins. His red hair shimmers.

"Better than a Rebel girl," I say.

"I want you by my side, India."

"I beg pardon?" I stutter.

"You are as smart as any boy at the university. You have only to learn from books as I did." Emory fidgets. He props a boot against the chair and cleans his shoe tips with a knife. Without looking up he says, "I would be so happy if you would . . . stay on. By my side. After the war, as a laboratory assistant, of course." He stops there.

I do not know what to say but stare dumbly at him. "When? When will the war be over?" I ask him. I avoid asking just exactly how this is going to be accomplished.

"Soon," he says. "Not too long. We will lose, of course. The North has as many soldiers as ants in an anthill."

"That's traitor talk, Emory!" I tell him. "Our generals are much cleverer than the stupid Yanks! We have won at Fredericksburg and Chancellorsville, too. Your father has placed stars all over the Virginia map. We are winning. General Lee has whupped that Yankee General Hooker's backside good."

Emory holds out his arms. Awkwardly he pulls me in toward him. "Don't ever believe that, India," he whispers. "Don't, please don't. We are going to lose. A quarter of our young men will be dead and another quarter maimed. And the old men will talk of honor. It is all such a lie."

I pout my lip but don't argue.

"There will be a new day," says Emory. "The war will be the end of more than slavery. Women are going to do all kinds of things they were never allowed to do. Right now there are women in the North demanding the vote. There'll be more and more of them parading and writing after the war. They'll get the vote. They'll pry it out of the men's hands. Women will go to college, own property, everything. You wait and see." He takes deep breath. "Most important, one day soon medicine will actually help people!"

I try and think of this new day. "Do you really want me to be with you?" I whisper. "Because, Emory, I have the money. I have the money to study at Oberlin."

"How can you have that money?"

"I just found it on the battlefield at Sharpsburg."

He doesn't ask how. He brushes his fingertips on my back as if I were a cat asleep in the sun. "How much?" he asks.

"Enough," I answer. "Enough to matriculate for one term anyway."

He drops his hands and turns away.

"My week is up. I must go," he says with bitterness.

"There will be a new battle very soon. There will be thousands of casualties again."

"Where? Here?"

"Only General Lee and his staff know. Did you know our side would have won at Sharpsburg, but a Yank found Lee's battle plans in a thrown-away cigar wrapper? This time he won't breathe a syllable of his ideas. God himself has no idea where Lee's going. He may try in the North somewhere over by western Virginia. People say he's heading for Pennsylvania."

Then as suddenly as he came, Emory is gone. He kisses his mother and his father and Ester. When only I can see, he throws a tiny kiss to me and then turns and gallops off in embarrassment.

I ride blind Maybelle to the Trimbles' every day after my morning chores at home. I am able to spend late morning hours and each afternoon at Longmarsh Hall. In the evening I am careful to attend to my mother. There is an understanding between Mama and me. It is not so much that Pa has died, but more that I have grown up years in one spurt. As long as I do my part I remain just beyond the boundary of normal Mama Rules. I also bring home food that we cannot afford and that Geneva silently packs each day in Maybelle's saddlebag.

Emory's work and my mastering of Latin give an even temper to life. It goes on much as it always has. The new world that Emory sees coming does not shade the color of May or June. Unending acres of blossoming, leafing, and fruiting orchards circle us. Somewhere beyond the green-gage plums lies the war.

One night after supper I go for a ride on Tom Trimble's horse. By the side of the river I see two pair of eyes winking like tiny stars. Here come a man and a woman, faces, hands, and clothes dark as mourning dress to blend unseen with the night. They rush by me, quiet as moths.

In a little black sling they hold a baby. His pearl teeth shine, and he smiles. He holds out one finger until his father muffles his attention away. Many evenings they pass by now, hardly parting the night air, freed slaves on their way north.

War's Beating Heart

July 6, 1863, the Winchester *Times* reports a slaughter in a place called Gettysburg, up in Pennsylvania. Seven thousand men die there. I try not to picture them. The paper says only that the dead have "passed" and goes on about the great cause we serve so gallantly in the South.

We hear differently from the survivors, who crowd into Longmarsh Hall on their way south from the battle. "Gettysburg was a rout," they tell us. "Our army is completely chewed up."

The only thing the paper prints that is not a lie is the list of casualties. Rupert Trimble is listed under the *T*'s. He was a lieutenant for only four days before the battle. His hat and sword are brought to Calvin and laid on the hall table by a subaltern. "He was shot defending a peach orchard," the subaltern pronounces.

Geneva sinks to the floor in the hallway. She covers her eyes and mouth. There will be no time for funerals or lying in state.

I find Calvin at the piano late one night, playing a lullaby over and again.

"Why?" I ask Calvin. "Why do they travel to Pennsylvania with thousands of men and attack each other on some alfalfa field they've never seen before, then leave?"

"It is the science of war," says Calvin with a sigh. "Lincoln is the enemy's leader. He wants to be reelected. For General Lee to strike at Lincoln in his own Pennsylvania would be a mortal blow to Lincoln's reelection plans and to the Union. If we had been successful, Gettysburg would have ended the war in our favor." Calvin plays a little trill on the upper keys of the piano. "As it happens, Gettysburg will finish us." Calvin explains very little more than that.

Longmarsh Hall becomes a field hospital. Geneva defers only to Doctor Hooks, who does daily rounds. Wounded men lie everywhere on improvised last-minute bedding. I try to pound down the nausea that hits me with every sight and smell, with the sounds the men make. I am hopelessly feeble in a sickroom. I am a useless priss the moment a bandage is off and the furious red hole of a wound revealed.

Doctor Hooks does the surgeries in the front garden atop a dining-room door with its four corners on dining-room chairs. When Doctor Hooks is taking a smoke I show him a letter from Emory. I tell him about the hospital notes that I transcribe every day. "I will boil your scalpels and the thread and needles you use, sir," I say. "Please allow me."

"Do you want to help these men or not?" snaps Junius

Hooks. "Get me some coffee for this man, India. And toss out this pile of bandages."

Out in back of the house I burn the bandages, as Emory has told me to do. The filthy smoke annoys Junius Hooks to no end. He comes around the back and asks me what I think I am doing making a fire with bandages.

"They are infected, Doctor Hooks. They are full of bacteria."

After that Doctor Hooks avoids me. Geneva takes me aside. "Junius Hooks is not about to change his ways, India," says Geneva.

"But it is what Emory does and says!" I insist. "Half these soldiers are dying of gangrene. It could be stopped. Some would live!"

"Doctor Hooks has practiced medicine for many years longer than you have been on earth, my dear girl," says Geneva. "Perhaps one day other men will learn other medicine and the world will change. At the moment Doctor Hooks is all we have."

Emory is given two short furloughs during the summer and fall after Gettysburg. Each time he brings me a haphazard clutter of surgical notes. I copy each one out, with its date and patient's name in clear longhand in a medical ledger book. The history of each man he treats, from the day of his admission to Chimborazo Hospital, is accounted for in detail. If there is a family on record or in the man's pocket papers, they must be notified. I write the letters and Emory returns with them so that they are mailed from Richmond and have some chance of being received.

Through the winter of 1863, when he is home, Emory loses himself in riding on the allées that crisscross the family orchards. He takes his own gelding, and I, in his cast-off trousers, ride Tommy's horse, Othello. Emory offers me his mother's sidesaddle, but I prefer to ride like a boy, astride. We canter fluently side by side through the identically pruned and fertilized maze of trees.

"One day, India," Emory tells me, "when you and I are long forgotten, people will ask the reason for this war. There used to be one. Now, the war has no reason behind it whatever. It just has a head of steam and a life of its own."

"There must be a reason," I say.

"Is there a reason if a comet flashes out of the sky and hits the earth destroying a whole civilization?"

No reason for this occurs to me.

Emory goes on. "I am a scientist. I believe only in what can be shown and proven. But I have begun to believe in Satan for the first time in my life."

"Satan?"

"Once it gets going, war has a brainless energy, India. It's got a beating heart all of its own. These horrible battles one after another are like a life force of rage that overcomes any kind of reason. My eyes tell me the war has shot up like boiling lava out of hell itself."

"From Satan?" I ask.

Emory answers, "The course of war is Satan's business, not God's."

"Well then, is God too weak to pray to, Emory?"

"No, God will prevail in the end," says Emory. He snaps his fingers. "One morning the war will be over. When the war's heartbeat stops, a white flag will be waved. There will be a great silence, then the birds will begin to sing again and no decent man would dream of shooting his brother because, from one minute to the next, shooting would become murder again."

We ride silently for a while and then Emory continues.

"It was father's hope," says Emory, "that one day it would be Tommy or Rupert who ran the family fruit business. Now there's no one to do it but me."

"Is it very hard to do?" I ask.

"You have to have an understanding of domestic botany, grafting, pruning, propagation, and disease management," he answers. "Fruit trees get blights and insect infestations and root rots. In addition you must have a head for business and the direction of staff. Father has it. I do not."

A tunnel of black walnut trees arches over us, perfectly spaced and tended so there is not a stray branch. Each tree was labeled by Calvin, when it was just a new whip, as to its species, age, and expected fruiting month, in indelible ink on tags of oil paper. It has always been Micah Cooley's job to oversee their care.

"Is there a book on the subject of fruit trees?" I ask.

"Yes, many," Emory answers. "Father owns a library of them. Why do you ask?"

"Because your mother is teaching me to draw. She suggests I paint vases of flowers. But instead I'm keeping a notebook. When I am not transcribing your hospital notes I draw the leaf and tree shape of each variety in the orchard and chart its progress from blossom to fruit over the weeks. There are hundreds here."

"Ten kinds of plums alone," says Emory.

"Damson, Black Ruby, Byron Gold, Homeside, Segundo, President, Stanley, Greengage, Blue Fire, Southern Star," I say.

Emory pulls up to a halt. He dismounts and, standing against the flanks of my horse, grabs me by the bare foot. "You have an amazing life ahead of you, India," he says, "a life full of things we can't imagine here in the middle of the war. But for God's sakes, if you stay here you can get killed. You must leave this valley, India. You should go to Kettletown with your mother's family and stay safe until it's over. There's terrible danger here."

I kick his hand away. "What more can they do? Even if the

Yankees came they would only steal peaches and plums."

Emory grabs again at my ankle and this time pulls me down from my horse. We tether both horses, and together we sit on a round rock and chew stems of grass. It is late December and the orchards are silent and leafless, but the sun has warmth to it and we enjoy it. Emory takes off his shoes. He says, "I've listened to a conversation with General Robert E. Lee himself."

"You have?"

"He visited my hospital. He has a bad heart, you know. He went to see the director, Dr. Preston Moore. Afterward, all the hospital mandarins went out for brandy fizzes with Lee. At the last minute they let me come because Mother is related to Lee's wife."

"What is Robert E. Lee like, Emory?"

"Modest. Almost sweet. A gentleman to the core. He told us what he learned at West Point Military Academy. He knows all the Northern generals from West Point."

"What did you learn, Emory?"

"Abraham Lincoln can only win next year's presidential election if he wins the war soon. Lincoln wants a new general. Lee thinks he knows who Lincoln will appoint. That man is ruthless, like an animal. He is a job drifter, not a gentleman like the other Union generals. Worse, he is a mean drunk. But he is a successful general."

"Who is this?"

"His name is Grant. This General Grant believes he will win the war by throwing a hundred thousand men at us and starving the Army of Northern Virginia so that it cannot fight. Lee says he's right."

"But how could he starve our army?" I ask. "He could never do that."

"Yes he can. He can burn the entire Shenandoah Valley. General Lee says if he were head of the army on the other side and wearing the blue instead of the gray, he would be forced to do the same to win the war."

"I won't leave here, Emory," I say to him. "I'm not going to Kettletown to sweep the floor and weed the vegetable patch."

Emory spits out his teasel of grass. "How old are you now, India?"

"I will be fifteen in two weeks' time."

"You are old enough to know well what the Yankee soldiers will do to the women here in the valley when they come. I don't want to describe what the Union Army ruffians and thugs do to innocent girls. I want Mother and Father to leave, but they won't."

"Fifteen is old enough to make up my own mind, Emory, and I choose to stay."

He lies back on the sun-warmed rock. "You have a year until you turn sixteen. Isn't that the birthday when you must throw away girls' clothing and wear corsets and hoops and speak only in giggles to young men?" he asks.

"I will never wear a hoop skirt or a corset in my life, Emory. They would have to hold me down and tie me to the railway tracks first."

"India, if General Grant is appointed general in chief of the Army of the Potomac, I will get word to Mother, and she will get word to your Kettletown relatives. You must leave. They'll come for you."

"Emory Trimble, I hate you!" I yell, and rip off a handful of burr bush and throw it at him. It sticks in his hair.

"I will not be here for your fifteenth birthday," says Emory. "If I were I would ask you to let me be the first young man to give you a kiss for the occasion."

"Oh, Emory, you're as dauncey as a bride! Just go ahead!" I say. "No one is watching, and if they were, they would not write it down in the book of sins!"

Emory's kiss stays for only the drawing in and letting out of a single breath, but it is warm and steady, as I have pictured it so many times when no one can read my unchaste thoughts.

MOTHER OF SINS

It is in March 1864 that the Winchester *Times* reports that General U. S. Grant will lead the Army of the Potomac. Geneva sees it in the paper before I can tear out the page. Word is sent to my uncle Peter in Kettletown. They pull their cart up to our house on Buckmarsh Street just as the morning sun comes out.

Peter is a stern man, big and bony. He speaks almost not at all. On the other hand, Aunt Divine is a maker of pronouncements. She leans forward always, as if to grasp the very next thing coming her way.

Mama offers her acorn coffee, although I know she has three bags of Yankee coffee in the larder.

Aunt Divine throws a look at poor Mama. She takes in how thin Mama is. Silently Aunt Divine is reckoning, *How helpless is Grandpa Moody? How much work is little Eddie?* She sees the unshaved whiskers on Grandpa Moody's chin and she sees the spots on Eddie's baby trousers. Aunt Divine computes every speck of my family that might make her life a misery, or will Mama and I contribute enough to balance things out?

"I have not told her that Pa is not coming home," I whisper.

"Can she work?" is the next question.

"She works her hands to the bone," I answer.

Uncle Peter says, "We will take the contents of the house." These are his first words to me.

All that Pa left in the world is here in the house. Boots near the wood box, hat on the post. Sweat stain on that hat around the crown. The harness he was stitching hangs on the wall. His shirts are folded neatly for him to return to them.

"Any silver to sell?" Aunt Divine asks. "Anything of value?"

She unearths the spoons and the silver teapot Mama treasures. Then she spots Pa's boots and the rest of his clothes. She folds up the shirt and vest that I still hide my face in to smell Pa's ever fading smell. I tell her, "No, please! Not those!"

"What do you mean? These will do Peter nicely," she says, and puts them in a trunk to take home. Uncle Peter hauls Pa's harnesses onto the wagon bed. Two boys help him put the furniture and every dish we own on the back of the wagon. Peter gives them a penny each for their efforts, and they make faces at him when his back is turned.

The house empty, Mama holds the bolt of scarlet velvet, which she has taken from its muslin bag in the back of the kitchen closet. Mama says her first words of the day. "I was saving this for India." She says this slowly.

Divine gathers the bolt of lustrous scarlet in her arms. "No decent Christian woman would wear a dress this color," she says. "Still, it's worth money. We will sell it."

"It's mine," I say. "Mama gave it to me for when I grow up."

"It will take more than a few pennies to keep and feed your family, India," says Aunt Divine. "We must be as one and turn from selfish thoughts."

I write on a card with a stick of stove blacking. In block letters I say, "Gone to South Pasture Road, Kettletown, W. Va." I stick it in the windowlight of the door. No use locking the door. We don't own a key anyway.

Aunt Divine sizes me up. "The Lord does not like pouters, India," she says.

"Yes, ma'am," I say.

"You are blessed to have Peter and me to take you in. The poor have no choices in life, India Moody. Without us you would be a refugee, starving like a homeless dog on the road." Aunt Divine adjusts the well-filled bosom of her dress. The gingham is tiny little green and black checks with a bleached white collar. No red there.

Blind Maybelle is tied to the back of the wagon and we commence our journey.

Aunt Divine sits next to me. "What's in that bag of yourn?" she asks.

"Books," I answer.

"Well you'll have precious little time for books, my girl," she declares. "Your mother and I will run the family business. We make 'White Jeans.' That's two pairs of cotton trousers every day, start to finish, and that pays the bills. Do you sew?"

"Not very well," I answer.

I will be expected to care for Grandpa Moody and Eddie and Mama. Aunt Divine tries to catch my eyes but I don't let her. Don't, for a moment, think Grandpa Moody and Eddie will take up the whole of my obligations, she tells me. I must cook for the family and care for their garden to contribute to the common purse. Food is scarce. Though we are kin, there's a cow to be milked every morning at six and wood and water to haul. Laundry to be washed and the dishes scrubbed.

"Is there a Kettletown school?" I ask.

"School!" Aunt Divine says this as if I had asked for a ride in a hot air balloon.

I pretend to listen to her list of Bible study and home chores. I pretend to agree. All the while, inside me a panic is rising. I listen to Aunt Divine's assignment of responsibilities.

"Get ahold of yourself, young lady," says Aunt Divine. Mama hears not a word of any of this. In times past Mama has been a tit-for-tat match to Aunt Divine any day of the week.

Clouds of flies lavish attention on the horses. Uncle Peter gives me a fly switch, which does about as much good as a wish. I pull Geneva's hat down over my eyes, which grow small as peas and more squinty with every passing hour.

Until the following day's evening, I sit next to Uncle Peter, breathing the dust of the road. The only thing to do is silently memorize every turning, odd tree, and trace of our course. At the end of the journey we are not better friends than when we started out.

The parlor and porch of Uncle Peter and Aunt Divine's house is entirely transformed to a sewing shop. Aunt Divine and Mama will cut and stitch an endless stream of trousers. These are made of heavy bleached cotton that is meant to last for years, they say. The trousers have chimney-pipe legs and are not cut to flatter a man. Twelve pair go into a brown paper parcel marked WHITE JEANS at the end of each week.

The cloth sits wrapped on great bolts at the side of the room. "Your mama is a first rate seamstress," says Aunt Divine. "You will have to learn to stitch as well as she. I don't know what you've been learning in the past year but it certainly isn't sewing." She takes my books and places them on a high shelf. She looks at the titles of my chemistry,

Latin, and botany as if they had come directly from the red rivers of hell. "You may ask for them when your work is done, India."

Other than the white cloth and a certain oil-dyed cotton called butternut, there is no material that can be bought in stores. We cannot import anything because the Yankees have sealed our borders. "They are taking the modern world away from us," says Mama. "All that we have is what is made by women at home."

"We are losing this godforsaken war and it can't be too fast for me!" I say.

Aunt Divine snaps, "That is unwanted commentary, India. If you look in your Scriptures you will find that it is a cheerful and submissive woman who walks in God's way. In the South we follow God's way without questioning. You wait and see, my girl! The Lord will provide for the South until we prevail!"

To pass the time, Aunt Divine sings from the hymnal. *Snip, snip*, go Mama's tailor shears. The two of them measure, cut on patterns, and sew the same pair of trousers every day over and over again. Who would wear them? Who would buy them? No one says, but once a week, the jeans are picked up by a stranger. Once a week a new bolt of cloth and twelve dollars Confederate scrip money is left at the house by a Department of Prisons driver to pay for their efforts. This is the family income. Every penny is discussed and hoarded before it is spent.

I rise before the family each morning, just at the sky's first graying. Last night's **stove ash**es must be taken out and spread on the vegetable garden. Dry wood has to be set in the cookstove fire and lit. If there is not enough of the right size for the stove, more logs must be split with an ax. If the ax blade is dull it must be sharpened on the whetstone. There is no wood or coal for sale during the war. Almost all heavy wagons and horse teams have been taken by the army, so wood can't be hauled or delivered.

When the fire is lit I heat a kettle of water for morning washing and go milk the cow. No one spies on me in the barn's warm stalls. I have a book of Virgil's poetry on my lap as I squirt the warm milk into my pail. While it fills I recite the Latin words, trying always to remember what they mean in English.

One morning Mama's eyes puzzle on me when we are alone in the kitchen. "Divine says Cy is dead," she says suddenly. "Divine said she is praying for Cy's soul."

"What?" I ask. I am alarmed. Doesn't Divine know Mama must come to this by herself? This news will give Mama hives and migraines all day. She could break down and become like she was at the Spreckles'. I could throttle Divine.

"Is it true, India? He is only away. He is not dead. He is soldiering. He will come back at the end of the war!" In her voice is the beginning of panic.

I know I can't pretend any longer. I go to the dresser in

my room. In its top drawer are the buttons. I bring them to Mama. I put them in the palm of her hand and close the fingers over them. "Captain Davis came by the Spreckles' when you were asleep. He gave me these."

She holds them without looking at them. Finally she whispers, "I sewed them on, you know. The night before he left."

"When the war is over, Mama, we will mark his grave. I know where it is."

She gets up and goes back to work without tears or hives. "I am glad you told me, India," she says.

"Are you going to be all right, Mama?" I ask.

"The scissors and the cloth comfort me," she says.

I sprinkle the floor of the house with sand and then sweep it clean of debris. When that is done and the bread set to rise, I come in to help Mama with Eddie and Grandpa Moody.

The only time away from the work is Sunday. The Church of the Second Coming has sermons twice as long as Berryville Presbyterian. The deacon is a woman, during this time of no men at home. Deacon Adele Conover will give a man a peck of trouble if he tries to retake his place after the war. She stem-winds on for a couple of hours about why God burns the unsaved in hell. Then there's singing and praying and healing. Aunt Divine, in her checked dress, takes the place next to me and makes sure I sit up with an arch in my back and kneel straight without leaning back lazily against the pew seat. I slip my Latin grammar into the casing of the hymnal and keep its pages hidden from Aunt Divine.

Outside the church the parish serves its own Sunday dinner to all. All war talk begins with how blessed we are to be safe here in Kettletown. In the Shenandoah Valley, everything of value has been stolen, killed, or set afire by the Yankees. There is nothing to eat in Winchester, all food destroyed by Union General Hunter, who chooses people's houses and burns them randomly. Union General Milroy has made a fortune stealing local family silver and sending it north to his own wife. When a Winchester boy calls him "Spoons Milroy" to his face he has this boy whipped in the public square. "The blood ran into the boy's shoes," says Adele Conover. "God save his little soul."

Bowed heads at Sunday dinner thank the Lord that we are on the fringe of war, not in its churning mouth. Kettletown is too small and poor to be noticed by anybody but horseflies.

One day a donkey cart stops in front of the house. I don't know quite what date we are at now. I believe it to be past May by counting Sundays since I have come. It is two months since I have heard anything of the outside world. An old colored man, with clouds of white hair, gets out of the donkey cart. He has brought walnuts wrapped in newspaper to exchange for our eggs. I unwrap them behind the chicken house.

The newspaper is dated June 20, 1864. Its single page is full of a new battle in a place called the Wilderness. Somewhere near Fredericksburg the fighting raged strong for three weeks inside a marshy woods. The swamp was set afire, and thousands of men were consumed, falling burned into the shallow waters. I read the paper thirstily. There is nothing more to know than what is on this one page. Although the paper won't admit it, I know the South will never rise again.

Aunt Divine and Uncle Peter have no comment except that the war is run by people who know more than we do. I look across at Mama, but she only bows low over her soup. *India*, say Mama's eyes. *We have no choice and no money. We must stay here.*

I am not staying long, Mama, say my eyes back to her.

In bed at night I wonder, Could a girl from my class of people walk in through university doors? What would the professors say if I recited a hundred compounds and their formulas? Would they say I was just a harness maker's daughter and make me go home to Kettletown?

I am allowed to read my books but never in candlelight because that is wasteful. I make our candles of twisted rags soaked in old melted wax. I wrestle with them while listening to Uncle Peter read the Scriptures. They are near useless. They fall over and burn up in less than a minute.

Emory has given me a book on plants in the Linnaean system of classification. I say the words "Cotyledon, dicot, angiosperm." I spell them aloud.

Mama finds me churning butter one afternoon, one of my few pleasant and quiet tasks. The stone dairy is April cool even on the hottest day in August. The motion of the churn paddle lets me recite the poetry of Catullus.

Mama hears me from the doorway. *"Furtivos hominum vident amores."*

"Are you speaking in tongues, India?" she asks.

"I am reciting poetry in Latin," I answer. "It is like the words to a song."

She sees how cut and calloused my hands have become from handling firewood, lye soap, and plow handles.

"You need a little orange oil for your hands," she says. "I will see if Aunt Divine will give you some."

"No thank you, Mama," I snap. "I don't need the time of day from that pinch-lipped prat!"

Mama slumps into the deep stone windowsill. She lays a pair of Eddie's torn trousers in her lap. She pulls the buttons to see that they are tightly sewn and do not fall off and get swallowed.

"India," she says, "what are the seven deadly sins, please?"

"Sloth, gluttony, lust, greed, wrath, envy, and pride," I recite quickly.

"And which is the mother of the other six sins?" she asks.

"I do not know."

"It is pride, India. Pride is your failing. Pride leads to all other sins, anger, greed, sloth! These are what Aunt Divine sees in you! You are proud and so you answer back to those who give you charity. You have uppity ideas of studying in a man's world. Uncle Peter and Aunt Divine can turn us out among the refugees on the road at the drop of an ungrateful word. We are penniless. You must swallow this pride. You cannot win a war with Aunt Divine, India. She will out-sharp you because she has the power," says Mama, and sits, holding her head.

Tears spring into my eyes, because Mama is right.

The summer of '64 has drifted seemingly forever until goldenrod begins to spill through the hayfields. One Sunday in August, Adele Conover pulls a letter from her basket. She places it in my hands.

"You will give me the letter, India," says Aunt Divine.

"But it is for me!" I say.

"You will give me the letter!" she repeats. "You have Sunday dinner to serve to thirty-four people. You may read the letter tonight when your work is done."

"It is my letter, Aunt Divine." I put it in the bosom of my dress.

"You have defied me!" she says, and shoots a severe look to Mama.

"Ma'am," I say, loud enough for the whole church to hear, "I shall serve dinner as I am bound to do. I will wait until my work is done to read my letter. But I am keeping my letter because it is mine."

"You will obey me, India, or you won't see the inside of one of your ridiculous books for a month!" says Aunt Divine.

A mist of perspiration beads up on Mama's face, and she falls forward in the pew. Soon she will lie in bed, curtains drawn against the blinding daylight.

"Look what you have done to your mama!" says Aunt Divine.

"Is it the migraine, Polly?" asks Adele Conover. Three pink-cheeked farmer's wives trot to my mama's side. They ease her to her feet and lead her to the church door.

"India," says Adele to me, "our son's got the fly cart out back of the church. You take your mama home and put her to bed. We'll take care of everything here."

I spear a doubtful glance at Aunt Divine.

Adele Conover follows my eyes. "Sister Divine," she says. "India Moody has served Sunday dinner without fail since before Easter. She has served us and served the Lord. Christian charity says she may be excused to take care of her mama, by the grace of God."

Aunt Divine's tongue moistens her lips and saves what she wants to say until later. Her eyes flash and her shoulders straighten as if for conflict. It will be the end of me in this household.

———————•◆•———————

I give Mama one of Emory's Salicin ampoules in a spoon of honey. Talking hurts, so she signals me to bring a cool pad to cover her eyes. I take her shoes off for her. She folds and unfolds a ripple of coverlet between her thumb and fingers. "Read me Julia Pardoe's letter, India," Mama asks. She lies rigid in her bed.

I read Julia's description of a house full of Irish servants and a stable full of healthy horses. Julia tells of sparkling visitors, piano lessons, birthday parties. Her mama and papa are well, and Alden is reading law at Oberlin College. Mama asks to hear it again. I am careful not to read Mama the last page, because it will break her eggshell heart.

Dearest Tiddy, I know some way you will find the money to pay for tuition fees. You have to pass the examinations in Latin, German, chemistry, biology. You must come as soon as you can to get ready for fall term! I don't know about trains. I don't know how you will get here, but I know somehow you will. There are many pleasant girls here in Oberlin but I love none of them and never will have a friend like you in the world. Come! Come!

"You are holding something back," says Mama. She takes the letter before I can pull it away, and reads the last page. I know it hurts her eyes something terrible. After she has finished we wait a long minute, listening to a conversation between two cardinals in the trees outside.

"There is nothing in the world like desire," says Mama. "Desire can't be stamped or beaten out."

"It is not going to be beaten out in me, Mama."

She sits up in bed, eyes half closed, and reaches under the mattress. "India, if you follow a life course outside what the Lord ordains I will never see you in heaven. We will be parted forever."

"Mama, I cannot live a life such as yours," I say as gently as I can.

"Oh, don't think I don't know! Your father told me he wanted you to follow your own path. He told me all about your studies with Emory Trimble and your ambitions, India. Just before he left with that Captain Davis he told me, *Polly, don't stand in the girl's way.*"

"Divine will throw me out, Mama. I see it in her eyes. So I will have to leave you. I will not see you for a while. Maybe not till I'm grown. I will miss you so much." My eyes prickle.

"Please write."

"I will write every week."

In that instant I decide very quickly what to do. "Mama," I say, "in money there is peace of mind."

"Money?"

"Yes." I go to the dresser. "Here. Keep this."

"What is it? Where did you get it?" she asks, shading her eyes from the light.

"At Sharpsburg," I answer. She knows how I came by it. She fans out the money.

"Under that red, red moon," she says. "Federal dollars."

"It was easy," I tell her. "It was morning. He was just lying there all so nice, just as if he was napping under a tree. His papers say his name was Captain Harry Price. He was shot in the temple. Right here." I point to my head. "He looked as if he just expired easy."

"You will need this money," she says. "You will need it more than I do, India. It will pay for that schooling you want."

"I can work off my college fees, Mama. Oberlin lets the poor students do that. I can't leave you, Mama, with such a heaviness of worry about you. The money will keep Divine in her place if she knows you are not a pauper. It means you can get away, Mama, if you need to."

"In God's eyes, you have committed thievery, India," Mama says. "This is stolen money."

"Use it, Mama. Use it for your peace of mind."

She lets out a sigh full of tears. "I cannot talk anymore. I shall be sick if I do," she says. "See what this war has done to all of us."

I circle my mother with my arms as I have not done since I was a baby. I talk to her as if she were the child and I the mother. "I will be safe at the Trimbles'," I tell her.

"The valley is all burned now," she says. "Everyone says so."

"I will be safe at Longmarsh Hall. Nothing will happen to Longmarsh Hall," I whisper again and again. Deep in her migraine, with her thin, vein-riven hands, she accepts my embrace.

"Be a good girl, Tiddy," she says. "Be a good, good girl."

THE TRUE COLORS
OF GOD

The air over the hillsides is heavy in my lungs. Will I ever see my family again? The road home is full of refugees. The war has sent them hundreds of miles away from their homes. It has split them forever with its lists of the dead. Maybelle frets underneath me. I am wary of the highwaymen who might cross my path. But to my surprise I run across Jimmy Ray Cox, now a courier for General Jubal Early.

Jimmy Ray is missing a hand. His left sleeve is tacked up in front to his chest button. He keeps an Enfield across his saddle, holding reins and gun at once. He tells me it is August 17, 1864, and sees me safely a day southward to our valley.

A Yankee picket shot his hand off. "I feel every finger on that hand I don't have no more. It does about drive me crazy," Jimmy says.

"Is it true," I ask Jimmy, "the valley is destroyed? People's houses? Just burned up for nothing?"

"Every time the Rebel army does somethin' General Hunter or General Milroy don't like, then they burn up someone's house and throw the family into the road as revenge. Now we got a new one. His name is Sheridan. He burned up everything left by Milroy and Hunter. Him and his men went through the valley like a dose of salts."

A few miles from the valley we smell the smoke. In the crackle-hard lick of the August sun I see the fences are scattered and gone. All cattle and hogs, chickens and goats, have been let loose. There are no horses left. They have gone astray or are stolen by the Yankees. Fields and barns, pastures and gardens, are ripped up or charred black.

Jimmy Ray Cox and I part company half a mile from Longmarsh Parish. Of course Jimmy can't wave. Instead he juts his chin skyward with a half smile, as if the wind will always be at his back.

The whole Trimble orchard has vanished. Every greengage plum, every Baldwin apple tree, is burned to black stumps in blackened ground. I spot Geneva, bending over some four-o'clocks in what is left of her garden.

"You are a sight for the sorest eyes, India," Geneva says. "How did you find your way back here? How did you get back alive with the roads full of bandits?"

I dismount and weep into my dirty hands. "The orchards!

The orchards are gone. Every tree." I throw myself against her wonderful bulk. Geneva wipes my begrimed face with her apron and herds me into the house.

In the kitchen she gives me some cold grits with a little precious milk. She tells about the time since Uncle Peter took me away in March. "Who?" she asks me, pointing out the window to where the first rows of stately pear trees used to grow. "Who did this? Who burned our trees and stole our horses? Who? Who killed our beautiful sons?"

She potters around in the shadow of the pantry cupboards and speaks as if she is discussing the weather. "Not long after you left, India, we had the news of the Wilderness. Another twenty thousand men on both sides dead in a filthy swamp, they say. I don't know how this can go on. I don't know why anyone lets it go on and on. Who keeps it going?"

I sit dumb at Geneva's words. I look at my folded hands. I don't want to know any more. "And Emory?" I ask as evenly as I can get my voice to go. "What has happened to Emory?"

Geneva turns away and stops the telling for a minute. She comes around the table and cluck-clucks at the dirt in my hair. She examines the condition of my hands and begins to work on the callouses in my palms with a pumice stone that she keeps in the kitchen drawer.

"Emory was with the medics behind the lines, filling in

for a late-arriving doctor. That much we know from his superiors at Chimborazo Hospital. A little ragamuffin from somewhere near the battle brought back Emory's field medical kit," she says. "It was found lying atop a stone wall on the Orange Plank Road. There was so much shooting from both sides on that day no one could keep track. Ten thousand men are still unaccounted for. Emory is missing is all we know. He was last seen pulling wounded men from a ditch. So he is missing."

I nod, as if this is neutral news. We know about the buzzards circling "the missing" on their leathery wings.

I am patient and wait for Geneva to say the rest.

At last she does. "There are a hundred perhapses and no Emory. If he were alive he would have gotten word to us long ago, India."

Without any permission my heart tears down its middle seam.

"God rest Emory's soul, and Rupert's and Tommy's," she whispers. Her words won't come out right. Geneva and I stay at the kitchen table, tracing its heavy oak grain with our fingers. We sit there until dark, and music from the parlor fills the quiet air.

"What will you do, India?" Geneva asks.

"I gave all my money to Mama," I say. "But I will still find my way up to Oberlin. I can work my way onto a scholarship. Emory would have wanted me to do this."

"My son had great love for you, India. He told me of his intentions the last time I saw him. Not that it matters now."

I dig my nails into the flesh of my palms but do not lift my eyes to Geneva's face.

"I will take his notes," I say. "The ones I was transcribing in the ledgers. I will take all his records of his medical work at Chimborazo and I will write them up as a paper. I will try and have them published somewhere. That's what Emory wanted to do."

From the front parlor drifts a war song. Calvin plays "Will He Never Come Again?" on the big piano. "His heart is bad after losing the boys," says Geneva. "He will be glad to see you, dearest girl."

I sit on the piano bench next to Calvin. His arm goes around me.

Above the piano is the map of Virginia, but its bright paper victory stars have all fallen off.

"We have lost the war. It didn't work," he says.

"I don't understand it," I tell him.

Calvin gives a bitter chuckle and trills his fingers up the keys. "In the end, the war was a rich landowners' revolution," he says dreamily. "Rich, arrogant landowners are always a part of yesterday, not of tomorrow. That's why it didn't work."

Then someone calls Geneva's name, faint as a sparrow, from somewhere in the house.

"Who is that?" I ask.

"His name is Patrick. The skin on both his hands is burned off," Geneva says, and she goes into the library.

Patrick is kept like a ghost in the hidden room behind the panel. He holds his hands up near his face, elbows crooked because they throb less. Patrick Reilly must be a year older than me. While Geneva changes his bandages he bites his lip against the pain. Geneva uses burn salve from Emory's field kit. She applies it twice a day and keeps the burns clean. I try not to look at Patrick's hands. "It is when we believe all doors are closed that the Lord tests us to find another door and open it," says Geneva.

Only Patrick saves Geneva and Calvin from a grief so entire that it could kill them like the typhoid. It is only Patrick that lets me take my mind off Emory for just a little bit of the day. Patrick is one of John Mosby's Rangers.

"There's a five-hundred-dollar price on my head," Patrick says. "The Rangers are like hot stoves. Don't touch us!"

"Why?" I ask.

"We ain't regular Army of Northern Virginia. We cut Yankee telegraph lines. We steal their horses and wreck their supply lines. We kill Yanks like rats whenever Yanks is out in small numbers. I got three officers with one piana wire!"

Geneva bathes Patrick, shaves him, and washes his hair in fuller's earth. She tells Patrick his raiding days are over.

He will never be able to hold the reins of a horse again, nor pull the trigger on a gun. He must think about gainful employment after the war. She says this exactly as if she were talking to Tommy or Rupert Trimble.

Before supper Geneva steeples her hands over the plate of dandelion greens and fatback. She thanks the Lord for bringing Patrick into their lives after taking their three sons away.

I say my prayers to the same God before bed.

"What kind of God are you, anyhow?" I ask rudely, on my knees, peering at the ceiling. "What the hell kind of God takes the life of Pa and Emory Trimble and burns the skin off Patrick Reilly's hands?"

God answers my profanity with Captain David Hunter Strother. Captain Strother and two Yankee soldiers ride up to the Trimbles' front door. He takes off his Yankee officer's cap and greets Geneva grinning, as if he had come again for Christmas dinner.

"What can I do for you, David?" asks Geneva.

"I am afraid I have come to burn down your house, ma'am," says Strother. He is ruddy cheeked and muscular as ever. I watch him from the peek hole in the front door. It is a long time since anyone in the valley has set eyes on a man in the pink of health. Every living soul in Rebel land looks like a weed in winter. Strother's gold captain's stars wink on the shoulders. His horse and his men's horses stamp and gleam like polished copper in the sun.

"David, go *on*," says Geneva.

"We know you are sheltering one of John Mosby's men," says Strother. "You and Calvin know right well what the price of that is. I will spare you arrest and leave you and your house in peace, but you must give him up. He will be hanged."

Geneva grabs hold of Strother's bridle and yanks it. "You may search the house!" she challenges him. "There's no Mosby men here."

Strother shakes his head. "Geneva Trimble, three of our officers came to camp at a gallop on Easter morning. They were dear friends of mine. They ran necks first into a piano wire stretched right over the Longmarsh upper trace. The wire was like a razor. Their heads were whipped right off their bodies! Those men were fathers of children, husbands of wives now widows. Reilly is a common criminal with a jail record for robbery and murder before the war."

"It's not my affair," says Geneva, "nor anyone in my household!"

"I'll give you one last chance to hand Patrick Reilly over." Strother bites off his words carefully. I sense that terrible temper that twitches right under the skin of his face. "If you do so, we'll leave you in peace, although by law you and Calvin should both go to prison as collaborators."

Geneva tosses her head. "If General Lee were winning this godforsaken war you would be hanged as a traitor!" Geneva barks, spittle landing on Strother's tunic. Her face is scarlet, her hair flyaway.

"Ah, but he is not winning," says Strother, smiling. "I believe the Lord in heaven has shown his true colors, and they are Yankee blue." Strother looks heavenward. "I know Patrick Reilly is in your secret little room with blood on his burned hands."

The color drains from Geneva's face. "There is no secret room!" she says.

"When Tom Trimble and I were boys we played there, madam!" answers Strother. He roars into the house, pistol first. Then I hear swearing, dirty words scattered all around the empty walls. Patrick has vanished through a small skylight window.

Strother pushes back past me. He comes outside to Geneva and throws a pair of boots in front of her. On the side of one boot the name P. REILLY is incised into the leather.

Geneva turns the boot over with her foot and then meets Strother's eyes with her clear and firm gaze.

"We loved him, David," she says. Her voice catches. "We've lost Emory, Rupert, Tom. Patrick came to us in the night with those burned hands. What could we do? We protected him and cared for him. Who will answer when all the bodies are buried in the ground? Tell me that, David! Who will answer?"

"Too late, Geneva," says Strother. He orders his soldiers to prepare torches. "I will allow you ten minutes to remove your belongings. Ten minutes only. Then the house goes up!"

"Calm your famous temper, David!" shouts Geneva. "Calvin has a bad heart. How can we clear the house in ten minutes?"

"Ten minutes," says Strother.

Geneva, Ester, and I try keeping Calvin down and outside, but he throws off our protests and begins to mount the stairs. "The letters!" Geneva cries. "All our family books and letters."

We pull and carry everything we can out of the house and onto the grass. Our clothing, the dishes, bedding, and a few light tables and chairs are stacked in piles. There are Geneva's mother's saved wedding flowers and her father's paintings of his horses. I pile Emory's precious notes from the hospital, and my transcriptions neatly on top of all his other papers and his books.

Calvin sits in the grass. His face is scarlet and his breathing rasps. He is trying to quiet his heart. I give him my handkerchief and turn away, as he is so embarrassed by his tears. He watches while I bring down the drawers of his cherry desk loaded with files and papers to safety on the lawn and go back for more.

"Every important document is here," Calvin says, satisfied a little. "The deeds to the property, my will, the transactions of our business for the last twenty years. All the pedigrees of the horses we gave to the Confederacy, so that we can be reimbursed by the army. But where shall they go? The first rain will ruin them!"

"Well it's all right for the moment," I whisper. "And we will find a place for safekeeping."

Strother keeps his eye on his pocket watch as if there was a three-legged race on. He raises his finger at exactly ten minutes. He does not give us another second.

Geneva begs to go in one more time. Strother whacks the side of his boot with a leather crop. He snaps at her, as if she were a misbehaving private in his army. "Geneva Trimble, you lied to me," he says.

Geneva pants air for breath. Sweat channels into her mouth. All the same she levels on Strother a hawk's stare. She cries into his face, "David Strother, you and I will live past this war. We will both survive it. And if you ever come back to Virginia, I will spread word of your destruction far and wide. You will be disgraced in the eyes of your neighbors, so help me God!"

Every word shoots out in a jumble of spit and fury. She snatches up his riding crop and whips his face with it hard, raising a welt across the bridge of his gentleman's nose.

He pretends not to feel it. But I see his face. I see the bulldog eyes and the cheeks gaining fire. "You are under arrest, Mrs. Trimble. For lying to a United States officer and aiding and sheltering enemy guerrillas. Arrest her,

Lieutenant. She'll go into the Louisville Women's Prison for a spell with the female collaborators. We will leave the old man behind in Winchester. He'll find friends there and they will take him in." He steps back. "That's the Moody girl, isn't it? She's been helping you out, hasn't she?"

He walks over to me and smiles. "I've seen you here before," he says conversationally. "Did you know I am an artist? I work for *Harper's Weekly.* You shall pose for me as the starving Rebel girl!" He steps back all mollyish, with one foot angled out from the other. David Strother squares his hands against his eye and frames me with them.

I spit on his boot. Strother laughs. "Oh, my," he says. "We need a little taming of the shrew!" His eyes sparkle with humor.

The men are waiting at the doorway of the house with their torches lit. Suddenly there is the sound of the piano. Someone is playing "How Many Jewels Will There Be in My Crown?"

"Bedell, is that you?" asks Strother.

"Yessir. This here is a fine piana, sir," says the soldier inside the parlor.

"I am a tenderhearted man," Strother says modestly, his eyes snicking from one to another of us. "That is a priceless Bechstein grand piano. We would need three more men and two hours to move it out and save it. Then the first rain would ruin it. Spare the house, Lieutenant. Burn only their possessions here on the lawn."

I try and save Emory's notes from the fire. A strong arm reaches for me and a soldier with a funny scotched-up way of talking stops me and pins me against him with my arm so I cannot move. He is a spade-bearded man, this hatchet-nosed Yank lieutenant, with eyes black as anthracite coals. He releases me when the burning is done.

Geneva and Calvin turn from the flames to each other. They sit on the grass and hide each other's faces in each other's shoulders. There is no sound from their grief, except the word "Who?" "Who will answer for this?" Geneva sobs, "Why burn my mother's letters? Why turn our beautiful valley into hell? Oh, tell me this is just a nightmare, Calvin!" She turns suddenly to Strother and asks him, screaming this time, "David, did you know that when you put on the uniform of an army you become Satan's child? Your work is Satan's work all in the name of God!"

I move away so slowly the men don't notice me. The horses' tack and soldiers' hardware jangle and clink. The men are blind and deaf to me. Once I'm out of their line of sight they forget me.

Geneva has seen me slipping away in the noise. She begins to sing "What a Friend We Have in Jesus!" There is a small note of triumph in the set of her back when Strother shouts, "Where's that girl? You let her out of your sight!" He swears an oath at them.

I don't return until the evening, when Strother and the soldiers are clearly gone.

When they leave there is no comfort to be had. There is nothing but tears and poking among the ashes with Ester. Not a page of Emory's notes, his observations of Shawnee cures, his proposals for new medicines, can be saved. The microscope is a blackened tube with its lenses blown out. Our brilliant colored crystals are as colorless as pebbles in the road. The three bow-fronted drawers of Calvin's cherry-wood desk are turned to cinders and Buddha is burned to a crisp.

"You come with us," says Ester. "We will take you in, Miss India."

Micah and Ester have a cabin you could get across in three strides. There is no room for me in there. The heat of the evening is intense, so I sleep outdoors. I pray for Emory and Geneva, and for Patrick, somewhere in this forest, burned hands, boots left behind. My prayers fall back on me like needles thrown into the air above me. I have as much faith in God as I do in a rabbit's foot.

How It Works
in Heaven

Micah and Ester work sunup to sundown, trying to yank some nourishment out of the burned ground. They tell me not to chop or hold the heavy handle of the plow.

"Your hands are not for fieldwork," says Micah Cooley.

I say my hands are no different from theirs.

I come upon a scrub pear tree, three-quarters burned, at the edge of the property and save ten pears. Sharing the pears at noon dinner, we suddenly hear artillery guns roaring and exploding somewhere nearby. It shakes us mightily, we three people, in the tiny cabin, but we say our fear to each other only with our eyes.

I believe Emory Trimble is right. Once a war begins it becomes as brainless as a tornado. Everyone knows the war is supposed to be because of slavery, but since Lincoln freed them after Sharpsburg, half the slaves have run away. Yet the armies keep fighting.

Micah Cooley laughs at my puzzlement. He says, "You

ever seen a big boy and a little boy fightin' in a school yard?"

"Sure, lots of times," I answer.

"Then you seen with your own eyes they don't finish it until the little boy cries enough!" says Micah. "And if he's too proud and ornery to cry enough, the big boy's gonna sit on him and mash his face in the dirt until the little boy's got two blind eyes and a mouthful of dirt!"

"That's us. The little boy," I say.

"That's us," says Micah. "The little Southr'en boy cain't do nothing but bleed. Black us, white us. It won't differ a bit in the South 'cause them that ain't dead is gonna have nothing to eat but spiders and snails."

"You be going back to your mama, Miss India?" asks Ester. She wipes her mouth carefully. Her eyes are on me.

"Maybe tomorrow," I say.

"No need to move on till the weather gets cold," says Ester. "Then we can't heat you or feed you no more. Your place is with your mama and family, Miss India," she adds.

I know that this is true. In the morning I pack my bag and get on Maybelle. I linger on her warm back as she grazes the cheatgrass, searching for something good to eat. Aunt Divine's face and the bolts of white cloth pass my mind's eye. I dismount. I crosstie some old ropes into a hammock outside the Cooleys' cabin. With an old oilskin I can fend off rain.

"You got any shoes, Miss India?" Ester asks.

"No," I say. "They fell to pieces."

"I have somethin' for you," she says, and plucks my sleeve to follow her. Ester takes me out to a trace that cuts deeply into the woods behind their cabin. It is almost invisible, being overgrown with suckerweed and fogged with insects. I follow her, ducking beneath a sheath of leaves and over a rooty, untrodden path. Ester is as sure on her feet as a dancer. She knows her way and steps boldly over the roots and fallen branches.

Finally we come upon what she wants. It is a pair of boots, soles mostly unworn, facing out at us behind a forgotten stone wall.

"This here one was a shrimp of a man," says Ester. The boots could fit me. The high tree cover is so dense the leather has been protected from rain, and it is not yet spoiled.

I lift the curtain of honeysuckle over where the legs of the owner lie. He is still all there, at least his Yankee uniform is.

"His belt is a good one," I say. "The canteen would be handy."

"He got a pack?" asks Ester.

"I can't see without moving the body."

"Get the boots off," says Ester. "Let's hope they come away clean. Otherwise . . ." Ester doesn't say what otherwise.

I kneel, straddle the legs, and yank one of the boots off.

It does come away clean, leaving a little cloud of dust in the air and the sock fallen on the ground. So does the second boot. I do not touch the socks.

Ester pokes under him, finds his pack, and yanks it out from underneath him. I ease him gently back into the leaf mold. His gun is rusted beyond usefulness and his ammunition pouch empty, but in the pack is a tin of bully beef. The canteen holds brandy.

"Good work," I tell Ester, and hug the boots. "He was a private," I decide. "Private Twoboots." The Yank private has better boots and equipment than our officers.

Ester sets the boots, pack, belt, and canteen in an orderly pile on the stones of the old wall. Then she rips up two sapling sticks, crosses them, and ties the cross with green bark strips. She places it on the man's chest. Ester falls to her knees. Her expression tells me to do the same. All the time I am aware that Private Twoboots could easily have been the one who set fire to the Trimbles' orchards.

"We are grateful for thy gifts, O Lord," says Ester. "Bless the soul of this, thy servant, and forgive us, Lord, our terrible trespass against his body." The rest of her prayer is said in whispers rapid as the talk of starlings.

Ester sighs big. "Miss India, y'all please never speak of what we done this day," she says. "When Miz Trimble come back home, she won't like one bit of this story." Ester looks away. She has read my thoughts. "They come back someday. No place else to go," she says.

We trudge on, pack and boots in hands. "You pine after Mr. Emory, is that not right, child?"

I nod my head because I cannot speak of Emory. I am as bad as Mama, hoping that "missing" might mean coming back someday. I can't bury Emory yet.

"Miss India," says Ester. "One day the Lord will call your name, and He will, because we all gets called. That day the hand of your pa and the hand of Mr. Emory will appear in a hole in the sky. Those hands will pull you up. I have seen this done with my mama, rest her soul. She was pulled up by the tiny hands of the children she lost on earth."

Ester spots blackberries that I miss. She's got eyesight like an owl. She hands me a handful of beauties and I swallow them one at a time. They stain my fingers purple.

"Pray every night, Miss India," says Ester. "Pray every morning for Mr. Emory's soul in heaven. The Lord hears our prayers."

"He hears us and a crowd of loudmouthed Yankees all praying at one time," I burst out. "Every night thousands of prayers from both sides flying at Him. What I want to know is, how can God sort it all out?"

By the stiffness in her back I can see Ester does not care for uppity white-girl talk about God.

"I give you this much, Miss India," Ester answers me. "If the Lord is on the South's side he is full of surprises."

I find Geneva's cache of stationery and a book of prewar

U.S. postage stamps in her desk. I write to Mama every week. To make myself laugh I draw funny pictures for Eddy and put them in Geneva's creamy vellum envelopes. "I am coming," I write Julia. "I am coming someday." I keep the stack of letters until I see some chance to get them mailed in the federal mail. One day this happens. I see Jimmy Ray again on the Berryville Pike. He is riding up to Harpers Ferry, which is just over the state line in western Virginia. He promises to post my letters. I give him a few apples that have escaped the fire.

Micah has taken it on himself to bring the orchards back to life, root by root and tree by tree. It is his own precious acres that he works first. On it were Belle of Georgia peach trees that gave the most delicate white fruit.

Ester and I prepare a rabbit for supper. She hangs the skin, ready to be tanned, on a fence rail. As Ester stirs our supper, a man comes into view at the boundary line of the Trimbles' north property. He crosses the cheatgrass like a distance runner. Ester stiffens up like a cat. We look for Micah, but Micah is three fields away.

Our four eyes are pinned on him. She says, "Commonly they go in pairs. Sometimes threes. The dangerous ones."

"I don't think he is dangerous. He's running from something."

We wait. He comes closer to the house, then into the yard by the pump. I look over his clothes and condition—

bad. He has blood and wheat hulls in his hair and smells of battle, sweaty clothes full of lice and fleas. Battle smell is easy to pick up, part cartridge powder and part fear.

"Puny white rascal," says Ester. The man's ear is torn in half. He wants water. Ester goes in the house. She brings out a clean rag and bandages his ear. He drinks until I think he will drown.

"There is a slaughter over the hill apiece," he says. "It's worse than a hog killing, but it ain't hogs."

I don't want to know what's out there. Ester has turned her deaf ear. Can we hear the artillery? He is on his way out of it before he gets to be the last man killed.

We don't know if he is Yank or Reb. Ester gives him a half bad pear. He eats it and spits out the seeds. Then he brushes his teeth at the pump. In a moment he disappears before we can ask which army he serves.

"He be too twiggish for a Yank," says Ester. "Yanks is plump."

Ester prays for the puny white rascal in her birdlike way, eyes squeezed shut, old knees in the soft sand. Then she goes back to the rabbit.

In my hammock under the same stars I sleep. In dreams heaven's system is revealed. Behind heaven's curtain the dead are absolutely not allowed to write letters or get onto the telegraph wires. They may visit us in dreams only. In dreams we are allowed to see them, every joint of the knuckles, every hair on the head. This way the dead may speak to those they love, here on earth, until we all go up there and join them. Pa visits often, but Emory Trimble never visits in dreams. Part of me pretends this means Emory is alive and well in some mysterious foreign university.

A four-day battle is like a twister wandering. It can explode anywhere inside a five-mile radius. This next battle sounds very far and then very near at different times. We feel strangely safe away in our dip of the hill, at the edge of the woods, but we do not know if a hundred bloody men will suddenly appear in Ester's potato garden.

Shells explode out of the redbud. Ancient and carefully engineered stone walls blow apart or shoot their rocks into the bushes. A mortar may or may not have hit the Trimbles' house. The laboratory and the piano might be cinders in the flames. But it could be safe as ever. Maybe the house is a Yankee officer's headquarters. We don't dare look or stray from the front yard of the Cooleys' cabin.

All the birds are gone out of the trees. I spend the day making a bow from a sapling. Micah has a lathe and three steel arrow tips. I fashion three arrows from hickory, straight as store bought. After two days I shoot a red squirrel fleeing on the road. I retrieve my arrow. We eat the squirrel at supper. It gives us each two mouthfuls of meat. Scrimpy food for days on end makes you weak.

Micah says the roots of the orchard will come back. I ask him if he has in safekeeping the deed to his own acres that Calvin Trimble gave him.

No is the answer.

"Where is the deed for the ten acres and a mule, Micah?"

"It were in Mr. Trimble's desk drawer with his own papers. We don't have no place for the safekeepin' of papers in this cabin."

Ester looks up sharply. There is fear in her usually silky voice. "That godforsaken desk and everything in it went up in flames," she says. "Our deed went up in flames! Micah, I thought you gave that deed to the bank!"

"I didn't trust no white man's bank," said Micah. "I trusted Mr. Calvin."

"Now ain't no white man gonna take your word about that deed, Micah."

"Mr. Calvin, Miz Trimble will come back," says Micah.

"They gonna be poor as church mice by that time, Micah," says Ester.

I say, "I bet Julia Pardoe's daddy filed that grant of land before the war. He was the attorney who drew up all the papers for Calvin. When I go to Ohio I will ask him to write it in a letter on your behalf. "

"Ohio?" asks Micah. "What for are you goin' to Ohio? I thought you was going to your mama in Kettletown."

"How you gonna get up to Ohio, Miss India?" Ester

shines up her spoon on her skirt. "General Lee's army spoiled all the train tracks and twisted 'em up like neckties. It would cost fifty, maybe seventy federal dollars to get t'Ohio from Harpers Ferry."

"How do you know that price, Ester?" I ask.

Ester examines the spoon. It is silver from the big house, rescued from the fire pile and cleaned free of char. "'Cause," she says, "it's what they charge the slaves what can't walk north."

"One of them dollars'd get me a fair-condition ax," says Micah. "I had a good whipsaw, but it was stole by the Yanks. We need wood to get us through the winter."

This is a reminder that I need to move on. The weather will come on cold. This little cabin won't keep an extra bird.

I haven't heard any artillery in a day. I think it's safe to go out. "We might get a couple of dead Yanks out of it. Maybe we could find us a Yank supply wagon. I could kill for real food," I say suddenly.

"The Lord don't like to hear that, Miss India," says Ester.

I listen out the window. I hear a few peewits in the trees. If the birds are back the soldiers are gone. I say, "I'll go out tomorrow. I'll hunt us up something to eat."

At the first gray streak of dawn Micah shakes me awake in my hammock. He will not tell me what he has found or why he wants me at this ungodly hour.

Jesus in Disguise

Everything is strangely silent around Longmarsh Hall. Two crows sit on the clerestory and caw at each other. Like a child's tantrum suddenly over with, there is a thick after-battle stillness in the air.

The first thing I notice is that the trumpet vines that frame the portico have been ripped away. Micah and I step in the front door silently.

The stench in the house is so shocking I believe no human being could stay inside for more than a minute. I force myself to cross the threshold and follow Micah. Men have camped out in Geneva's front room. They have not cleaned up after themselves. The house echoes grievously in its emptiness. If its beams and joists were the body of a person, no doubt it would bleed or cry. Micah beckons for me to follow him upstairs to the master bedroom. One look inside and I run for an open window.

Micah calls me back in. "Stay and the worst'll go away," he says.

In Geneva and Calvin's bed a man is lying. He is wearing a blue tunic.

"Dead Yank," I say.

"He is alive!" Micah insists. Micah holds a small mirror under the man's nose. The mirror clouds timidly with come-and-go mist no bigger than my fingernail. Micah has Private Twoboots' canteen. He spills brandy into a spoon and lets that dribble into the man's mouth.

There's a U.S. Army medical field kit on the chair. The Union Army gives its doctors newer, brighter instruments than in Emory's kit. They are set in neat velvet-lined compartments. Parcels of medicines lie underneath. Emory would know what to do with them, but I do not.

I tie a rag around my nose and mouth. It doesn't much help. Micah and I work without talking, stripping the man bare. There is no resistance in his body. Micah pulls the filthy bedding from under him and throws it out the window. The smell improves in the room. Then Micah bares the man's legs. One leg is gone, having been taken off at the hip. I leave the room and stand in the hallway, leaning out the window, sick as a cat.

Micah brings me back with a rag soaked in oil of cloves, placing it under my nose. "Easy," says Micah.

"I can't look at that missing leg again, Micah," I tell him.

Micah washes the man and pieces together one of the ruined mattresses. We lay him out on it. After more water and brandy he makes little *mew mew* sounds.

While Micah works on what I can't look at, I have been studying the lieutenant's face close-up. His uniform buttons say ELEVENTH VERMONT. I look sideways at the hawk nose and the spade-shaped beard.

"We can't do no more," says Micah. "Miss India, you better-should get the doctor or this man will die."

"Micah! Do you know who this man is? He's Captain Strother's lieutenant. Those men burned every precious thing! He burned the deed to your land and all the Trimbles' possesions!"

"He was followin' his orders," says Micah, pointing me back at Doctor Hooks. "He will die without the doctor, Miss India."

I complain, "There's a battle on. I'd have to pull Doctor Hooks out of the First Baptist Church in Winchester with our men dying in the pews right this very minute. He's not coming five miles to Longmarsh for just some old Yankee soldier."

Suddenly Micah's two big hands pick me up by the shoulders and hold me firm as a little hen. "Miss India," Micah says, "did not Abraham in the Bible welcome the strangers into his house? Didn't the Lord not say, 'Be not forgetful to entertain strangers, for thereby some have entertained angels unaware'? Is that not what the Bible says? How do you know the man in this bed ain't Jesus hisself in disguise?"

"I don't know that, Micah," I admit.

"I'll tell you another story you don't know, Miss India. Ester and me have a son. His name is Caesar, after the king of Rome. He was sent north with my sister when he was born. Caesar Cooley serves in the Union Army."

I do not know what I should say. I am exhausted by the sides of this war. Why did I ever think that the Negro people were pulling for the South? How could I have thought that for a minute?

A little corner of paper peeks out of the pocket of the man's tunic, cast on the floor. I pull on it. It's a letter. I pull it out and read it to Micah.

Dear Dady,

This is Seth and I can wright now and miss you. These are my letters in my oun pencil. Please come home fix the goat pen. Love, Seth B. Bedell

Dear Pa, Please pleass pleeze come home to us now. I speld pleeze three ways so one way will work. You have been in the armie for nearon five years and that is more than Mr. handley or anyone else so just walk north and take the train to home. I am doing so well in school my teacher give me the priz. Love and kisses, yr. daughter Anne Bedell

Dear Dad, I'm hopeing you are fine. We have the Mccauley's cow. Mama wants to send you icecream but it

wood melt on the way. Did you get the box of books and the
fruitcake and the medecins. We sent them to Hapers Fery.
I love you dady and we want you to be home for my birth-
day. Love from your son Henry jr.

Micah has nothing to say but just blinks across the bed
at me. I sigh. "Well, I maybe could get the doctor up here if
I tell him we got a Reb officer. If I lie like a rug, he might
come," I say.

In the stillness of the bedroom I suddenly hear my pa's
voice without mistake. *"Don't dawdle, India. Get the doctor.*
That man's wife and children are sending prayers up to heaven.
Those prayers are falling on you. Falling right down like rain.
Hear them!"

I run downstairs and tack Maybelle up. I get her to trot
smart all the way to Winchester.

Around midnight Doctor Hooks trudges up the stairs.
First thing out of Junius Hooks's mouth is, "That ain't no
Reb captain, India. That's a Yank if I ever saw one. Look at
his teeth. There's an army dentist been putting silver fillings in those teeth. He's an officer, too. Only officers get
silver fillings."

"He's got three children," I begin.

Doctor Hooks is snappish. "I've got five hundred thirty-
nine of our boys down on the floor of the Baptist Church
calling me by name. This one's a Lincoln hireling. Set this

whole beautiful valley on fire and destroyed it. I should walk right out, India Moody."

"Yes, sir. I have a letter from his children up in Vermont," I say.

Henry Bedell is still in his body. His eyes alone seem to live, swimming in their sockets, deeply black as winter night. Doctor Hooks asks him his name. Henry makes an effort with his lips but cannot form a word.

"When did this happen?" asks Doctor Hooks. "How many days have you been in this room?" He takes the man's hand. "Count me out in fingers. Count it out."

Henry Bedell counts three, then four. He doesn't know.

"Four days you've been up here?"

Eye blink for yes.

Doctor Hooks gives him quinine, from the kit, by mouth. Then he lifts the sheet and draws a sharp breath at seeing where the leg came off. He soaks a rag in chloroform and slaps it over Henry Bedell's nose. He asks Micah for turpentine and rhubarb powder from the medical kit.

I leave the room. I go to an open window just to get the all-overs out of me. It takes the doctor longer than I think it might. Then Junius Hooks strides out wiping Henry Bedell's blood off his fingers onto his trousers.

"The angel of death is at hand," says Doctor Hooks. "But I did what I could."

"Does he have a chance?" I ask.

"This was a field amputation," Doctor Hooks answers. "Done by a pretty fair army surgeon in the middle of the last battle. This man has been without water or care for some days. Not one field amputation at the hip has ever lived so far as I know of." Doctor Hooks slaps his leg. "I inserted a handful of live maggots into the open wound and closed the flap of skin over it."

"Maggots?" I ask.

"Maggots eat up morbid tissue, that's why," the doctor grunts. "I used that needle on the dresser. Can you spare the needle? It's good and new," he asks.

"Take it," I say. Before Doctor Hooks came I sterilized the needle in a flame.

"Some of the bad humors are out now. He needs water. I wish I had more quinine. I wish I had clean lint and bandages. Give him broth if you can find something to make it with. But it won't differ. He'll be dead by sunup because he's too weak and the fever will kill him."

"Sure about that?" I ask.

"Sure as tomorrow," says Junius Hooks. "Tell Micah to bury him quick or the house will stink like a morgue forever." Doctor Hooks spits into his hands and cleans his tired eyes. "Wouldna come up here if I knew it was a damn Yank."

"He's got those children," I say lamely.

"Yeah, girl. So did Geneva and Calvin Trimble. This dirty Yank might've pulled the trigger on 'em."

Then Junius Hooks chucks me under the chin. "India Moody?" he says.

"Yes, sir?"

"If by some miracle this man lives you must report him to the Berryville militia. The Home Guard. This fella's whole regiment is up in Harpers Ferry now, waitin' around for their next chance to raid us down here. This man is an enemy soldier. An officer. He is worth two of our men in exchange. Do you understand that?"

"Yes, sir."

"Or you'll be in trouble up to your ears. There's angry, hungry men hereabouts like to tuck it to a Yank and anyone helping him out. Women and girls got no business in war. They've got nothing but romantic notions."

"Yes, sir."

He looks at the shiny instruments in the Yankee medical kit admiringly. "Y'all won't be needing this kit," he says.

———◆◦●◦◆———

There is the tiny silence of Henry Bedell himself and the great big silence of coming death. Micah and I sit with both silences. Death in a room sucks daylight right up out of the air in front of your eyes.

"We have that tin of bully beef," Micah says. The beef, portioned out over a week by Ester was intended to save our own lives.

"I'll get it back at the cabin," I say.

"Ask Ester to give you my blanket, Miss India."

Ester folds up the blanket. She makes the beef tea and puts it in a bottle. Henry has to be slanted up on his doubled-over coat, since there are no pillows in the house. In the time it takes for the sun to close the day Henry drinks down the beef tea. When he is finished I go get my doll, Abby. In the bodice of her dress is a tin of steel-colored lozenges. They are Emory's Salicin pills meant for my pa. Pa's life was supposed to be right there in those ampules. I bring the tin into the room and give Henry his first of twelve German pills.

Henry struggles against the insults of pain. His hands flutter on the blanket. His lips make sounds but no words. I don't think he sees us, but he does not die in the night.

In the morning I give a second pill. His fever has gone and his face is cool. "He ain't going to last long 'lest we feed him up and dress that wound," says Micah.

"How can we do that?" I ask.

"His unit's skipped up to Harpers Ferry," says Micah. "The whole Yankee army's up there. One of us gotta go there and get some food and medicine or this man's dead as a donkey."

"You, Micah," I say.

"A lot of hungry people in the valley would kill a colored man for helping a Yankee soldier," says Micah.

"I'm not going to tell any neighbors, Micah," I say.

He shakes his head and grips his face in his hands a second. "Miss India, no white man in the world is gonna listen to no Negro or do nothin' he asks for. Even a Yank. What do you think them Yanks fought this war about? You think it were to free the black man?"

"I don't know, Micah. I don't know what the Yanks want."

"Don't ever think no white man is gonna die for no black man. Never gonna do nothin' for no black man 'cept cheat him. That's a pure fact," says Micah.

Micah gives me his old Indian saddle for Maybelle. Maybelle and I ride close against the Berryville Pike to Harpers Ferry. I stop to rest in Charles Town at the home of Tom Bowlen, a regular customer of Pa's harness business. Peggy, his wife, greets me at the door. She has gone so thin that her dress hangs on her as if it belonged to another woman. She shares an ashcake with me, which is all she has for supper.

I carry water for her and weed the garden. The four Bowlen horses, perfectly matched Belgians that took first prizes at the county fair in days past, are all gone, taken by the army.

I stable Maybelle in their barn and find an old flake of hay for her. The tack room door has escaped the notice of the Yankees. On a rusty nail set in the back side of the door is a set of four-in-hand lines and a driving bridle made by

Pa. I find the brass plate that attaches the head and side straps of the bridle. It has Pa's initials, *CM*, like all his harnesses. I hold it tightly in my hand, as if I could just touch a little bit of him.

I am on my way before the first bird of the day. I come down to Harpers Ferry from Bolivar Heights. It appears the whole Yank army is here in hundreds and hundreds of white canvas tents, set up like houses of cards in even rows. Downtown the flag snaps over the Magnus Hotel. It is the Stars and Stripes, unseen in the South for four years. Blue uniforms are everywhere I look, marching and lounging, playing and sit-staring. Yanks of every description are on the street. I am unused to the clattering of activity.

A soldier in the guardhouse asks me my purpose. My heart skitters.

"I have come to see the provost marshal," I answer. "I have news of a Union officer wounded and alive."

"You and four hundred other women," he snorts.

I lead Maybelle down Depot Street, hitch her to a post, and wait in line until my stomach hurts with hunger. The provost marshal is a busy man.

Finally he yells "Next!" and the woman behind me shoves me forward. "Get up there, girlie, and get it over with," she says.

I have the letter from Henry's tunic. I have his billfold

with his army papers and two dollars federal, untouched. I place them on the desk in front of the officer.

"Yes? What?" he asks briskly.

"Sir, we have a Union lieutenant in a house in Longmarsh Parish," I say. "He is badly wounded and needs food and medicine."

"Who is we?" asks the provost. "State your name."

"India Moody. Me and Mr. Micah Cooley, a freed colored man, have found Lieutenant Henry Bedell. His leg was amputated off, sir. He's still alive but not for long. If you send down some medicine and some food maybe we can save him."

The provost has smarty-pants eyes and a mustache waxed perfectly into matching points. I feel his gaze on me. He mocks a woman's falsetto drawl. "We got a sick Yankee we's tendin' and we needs food!" He comes back to his own voice. "The United States Army can only give to legitimate, provable Union soldiers who may be trapped and wounded behind enemy lines. You could have took that letter off a dead body. I can't believe all of the stories, missy. Nine out of ten are lies."

"But there's two good dollars in his billfold! If I was lying I would for sure have taken his money!" I hear my voice whine upward.

The provost makes a little scoffing sound and pushes the wallet back to me. He looks through his files impatiently.

The woman behind me starts to make impatient noises. "Get on with it, lassie," she prompts me. "Nobody ain't got all day!"

"Henry Bedell," reads the provost from a paper. "Eleventh Vermont Volunteers. Light infantry. Promoted to lieutenant last year. Field amputation at the hip September eighteenth, 1864. Reported to this office four days ago. Lieutenant Bedell was left in the company of two enlisted men who have since returned to camp here. They reported officer Bedell died on September twentieth of his wounds. Miss, I believe you have found the body, stripped it, and brought his effects here in the hope of cadging a little food. I know you people are starving down there in Virginia, but it is as the president and the good Lord have willed it. If you want something to eat go take the oath at the next office. They'll feed you something at the commissary."

"But it's not true! He's alive!" I say.

"You're lying," says the provost. "Next!"

The woman behind shuffles up. I press her back.

"I am not lying!" I say.

"You are lying," repeats the provost. "And I'll prove it." He pulls a certain paper out from Henry's file. "This is the test that never fails," he says. "If you lie to me a second time, young lady, you'll spend a night or two in our women's lockup for being a suspected spy. Do you want to try this test? Do you want to risk prison?"

"Yes!" I say.

He smiles with one corner of his mouth. "Very well." He smirks and—I can tell, for not the first time—calls out, "In my hand is the lieutenant's enlistment and medical record. Tell me," he says, "what color are Henry Bedell's eyes? Blue? Brown? Green? Or something in between?"

"Black!" I blurt out. "Black as the ink on that paper."

A change comes over the provost's face. "No one can fake that test," he says, "because no one lifts a dead man's eyelids." The officer makes the woman behind me wait. "Lieutenant Bedell was a very popular soldier," he says in a softer voice. "His men will be anxious to hear of him." He scrawls something on a paper and hands it to a private at the doorway. "Give this to Major McCarthy," he says. "Major McCarthy is the senior officer of Bedell's unit."

My Prisoner

Micah and Ester unpack the bags that the Eleventh Vermont has sent to their lieutenant. Each item is picked out of its wrapping and placed on the kitchen counter like the treasures of Captain Kidd.

There are meat pies and lemons and whiskey. There is butter and flour, molasses and coffee, real tea, oranges, and ten tins of beef stew. There is soap and lamp oil and a toothbrush. They have packed quinine for pneumonia, laudanum for pain, bandages.

That evening Henry speaks. "Thank you, miss," is what he says in a Yankee whisper. He takes a whole cup of beef tea. I give him his medicine with laudanum for the pain.

After another day color returns to Henry's face. He dictates a letter for his family. I write it while Micah changes his bandage. He stares at the ceiling of the Trimbles' bedroom. Someone has written dirty words on the wall. There is a hole burned into Geneva's red-and-blue Persian carpet on the floor.

"I am ashamed of my army," he says. "We came to free the slaves, and all we've done is ruin your beautiful valley and humiliate your people. I have burned the contents of this house with my own hands."

"It's the way of soldiers," I say drily. I cannot feel anger at this man.

Henry makes a helpless gesture. He examines his fingers and finds them clean, the nails scrubbed by me, just as I used to do for Pa. He says very low, "I recall marching down the Main Street of Westfield, Vermont. Bands playing, flags snapping in the wind. It made us boys all feel so pure of heart, every last sinner among us. Then we all saw the inside of the war. All that pure-hearted palaver meant nothing."

"Same lies, different flag, here in the South," I say.

It is I who prepare meals and Micah who cleans the wound. In the light hours Micah must tend his orchard roots before winter. He spends the long days in the fields. Henry's mates have given me a pistol, and it is never far from where I am. One morning Micah brings me two big Ys of hickory sapling. Henry and I use his barlow knife to fashion them into a pair of crutches. He likes the work and accomplishes it with fair skill.

"What will you do?" I ask.

"I will go back to my family, if I can make it over the line to Harpers Ferry. I owe my life to you. I wish you would come to Vermont until the war ends."

"I would be homesick in the North so far away," I answer.

Three times I return to Harpers Ferry. Each trip I have a Remington pistol stuck under the pommel of my saddle, and I am not so afraid of bandits on the road. I mail my letters, although Mama never can send a reply because mail can't be delivered to Longmarsh anymore. Each time, the men in Henry's unit pile Maybelle with whiskey, bacon, and tins of beef.

When I return from my third visit to Harpers Ferry, Henry has slithered and bumped down the stairway and is seated at the piano, playing.

"I'm actually the choirmaster for the First Presbyterian Church of Westfield," he says, and arches his hands deftly over the keys, playing the doxology. I have not really heard music in two years. I can fairly breathe in the melody. For a while I forget the odor of smoke that carpets the ruined land and clogs the lungs.

Henry's songs, pounded out on the Bechstein as if it were a church organ, are always hymns or battle marches of the Yankee army. One day he and I move into the glass-house. It is warm and relaxing for him. Emory's plants still live in their pots, watered by rain through broken glass-house panes. We look out at where the south orchard was. Henry is able to sit in a rocker. "What was out there?" he asks me. "Before the war?"

"Peaches," I tell him. "Plums and grapes and apricots, apples in the fall."

He finds a piece of cryolite on the table. "What is this? What was this glass house used for?" he asks.

I show him the few scraps left of Emory's notes and studies. "All the rest were burned," I say. "I used to help Emory Trimble. He tutored me, and I was reconstructing all his work in order to have it published. There is a Doctor Lister in Scotland who is doing the same research. Emory wanted to beat him to it!"

"Will he not reconstruct his papers and his knowledge after the war?" asks Henry.

"He is missing," I answer.

Henry cocks his one boot. "Where? When?" he asks.

"Wilderness. There's ten thousand missing both sides."

"Wilderness was the worst battle of the war," says Henry. "Missing's bad after a time passes," he adds.

"Missing's dead," I say.

Henry works the crystal back and forth in his fingers.

"How about you, India? What will you do?"

"I will take Maybelle and I will ride to Oberlin, Ohio, where there is a college that accepts women. I will work my way through on the college farms. I will obtain a degree and set myself for natural philosophy."

"Natural philosophy?" asks Henry.

"Men's science," I answer. I take the crystal from his

hand. In the drawer are fifty more cryolites. I skim them from the drawer to my lap. "On the way," I say, "I will stop at Sharpsburg where the battle was. There's a church there near where there used to be a cornfield. My father is buried on the north side. I'll mark his name in the ground with these stones. Someday I'll bring my mama there so she can see it properly and say good-bye."

Henry stares out the window. When he returns my gaze he says, "Ohio'll be five hundred miles. Take you half a year to get there. Bad roads and bad men all along 'em."

In the kitchen, as of old, Ester sings a Gospel song as she stirs navy beans. From the parlor Henry plays "Maker of Earth, to Thee Alone."

On my return from Harpers Ferry in the last week of October, I carry a letter for Henry. He opens it at breakfast. A true, rare smile crosses his face.

"What is it?" I ask.

"My wife, my family, are coming down by railway to Harpers Ferry. They will take me home at the end of November," he says. "I should be strong enough to cross the border of Virginia by then."

"We will hide you in Micah's mule cart," I say. "We'll put you in a burlap feed bag and take you over."

At that very moment Grace Spreckle suddenly taps on the window of the parlor like a woodpecker.

"Yoo hoo!" Eloise calls. She moves on in, her sister following. "I smelled bacon and coffee out on the road for the first time in a coon's age!" says Grace. "Is that bacon and grits I smell? Is that coffee?"

In an instant the sisters fill up the quiet house with their chatter. "India Moody, if it isn't you, plain as day!" says Grace.

They look everywhere and cluck over every stained rug and broken chair like a brace of terriers. "We were just passing by the road!" Eloise says. "And Grace says to me, 'Sister, isn't that bacon and coffee I smell coming right from the Trimbles' kitchen?' Then lo and behold, Grace looks in the kitchen window and sees Ester eating a plate of flapjacks and bacon that hasn't been seen in the valley for three years! So here we are!"

I smile and walk out of the kitchen. Henry has vanished into the library and the hidden room at the first sound of a strange voice.

"Now tell all, India Moody!" says Grace. "Why are you not with your mama in Kettletown? How did you really get this wonderful food?"

I serve out a plate of grits and bacon for each Spreckle sister. "I found a Yankee supply wagon," I tell them.

They don't believe me for a minute. "You *are* the lucky

one!" chirps Eloise. For just a few moments all concentration is on eating. The Spreckles have always exhibited the most delicate of table manners, remarking with raised eyebrows on the table manners of all around. They cannot keep that going after months of eating corn mush and ashcake. They take three fills of their coffee cups each. They are giddy with it.

"We want every detail, India Moody! Where did this feast really, really come from? Supply wagons don't have fresh eggs and bacon. We want to know what's going on up here! Does your mama know where you are? How'd you get this bacon and grits? Even General Lee doesn't have bacon and grits on his plate anymore."

"I found it. I found it after the last battle by the side of the road."

Grace's eyes narrow. "You can tell us, honey! Who've y'all got in this house, India Moody? Who's that playin' 'Battle Hymn of the Republic' on the piano in the afternoons? Not you! Your mama says you don't have a musical note in your little finger."

I can't think fast enough to answer this right. If I can't keep Henry secret I'll be sent to Louisville Women's Prison for sheltering a Yank and—sweet Jesus!—it will go badly for Micah and Ester. "Search the house!" I say. "There's no one here. It's Micah who's playing piano, if you want to know."

Grace Spreckle takes me by the hand. "Dearest India," she says. "We think we know who is in this house. We think we know *where* he is in the house. Many years ago, before you were born, Calvin Trimble changed his will and Eloise and I just happened to be in the library when Geneva goes by and poof! She pushes a little lever—"

I interrupt them. "He's my prisoner," I say. "I am getting him well and then I'll take him up to the Yanks and exchange him for Geneva Trimble. That is my plan."

The sisters exchange loaded glances. Grace pipes up. "Geneva Trimble is no more in prison than you are, dear girl. Captain Strother lost her on the Winchester Railway Platform."

"Lost?" I ask.

"It was very exciting!" says Eloise Spreckle. "Captain Strother personally took charge of Geneva Trimble. He tied her hands behind her back. She was pushed in with a passel of ruffian women, thieves and strumpets and so forth. They were all waiting on a siding to be herded onto that prison train bound for Louisville. Geneva slipped one of the girls a silver hair comb. Just like that, the girl untied her and Geneva was gone. Imagine! Both Geneva and Calvin are safe, dear girl. We know where they are, of course, but naturally we promised not to tell! Captain Strother has vowed to find her, but he'll never hear it from our lips!"

I am too stunned to know what to say. Grace takes me by

the wrist. "Now look here, India. Prisoners are the business of the Berryville Militia. Your mama would have a fit if she knew you were sheltering a Yankee fugitive!"

Eloise does not entirely agree. "Hush, sister!" she says. "This is exciting, India. Can we meet him?"

Grace says she would give all the tea in China just to hear that snurled-up Vermont lingo. They want to hear him talk. They want to know what his wound is like and what we are doing to heal him up. They want to know if he is a gentleman or riffraff.

I go into the kitchen, get a tablespoon, and pull the cork out of the bottle of whiskey that Henry's unit has given me. I give the sisters a tablespoon each in eggcups, just like they take at night. "This is good sipping whiskey," I say.

"I'd like to get a little more of that. Against the winter coming," says Eloise.

I give them the whole bottle and some precious coffee and eggs. "More where that came from," I tell them. I bargain with them. "If anyone tells about the prisoner," I say, "if word gets out, then I'm finished. And no more brandy, eggs, or coffee."

"We won't tell a living soul! It is too exciting for words!"

"Our lips are sealed! Y'all rest-a-sure as the sun rises!" they chime together.

But Henry does not rest assured. All day he frets about

it. "I am so close to getting home and yet so very far away," he says. "Like a man who can just reach out for the lifeline when he has fallen off his ship. I will walk tonight on my crutches up to Harpers Ferry. I would rather die in a hayfield than be taken to Libby Prison."

Micah and I try to talk him out of it. He settles for staying the night, hidden in my hammock in the trees. We cover him with oilskins and wait for morning.

Then, unasked for, Doctor Hooks stops by just at moonrise. "I came to check up on my patient," he says.

"Gone," I say. "You can look."

"I don't believe you." Junius Hooks tramps through the house. He finds nothing at all. He pushes the lever to rotate the library panel. There is nothing in the room. How does he know about it? The Spreckles have told him. The Spreckles who promised Geneva they would never say a word.

"He is gone," I repeat. "The militia came at suppertime and took him away."

"India Moody, are you lying to me?" says Doctor Hooks.

"No, sir."

"Who-all in the militia came?"

"I don't know who. Three men in gray coats is all."

"If the militia don't have him, India," says Doctor Hooks, "they're going to find him come hell or high water. You've run out of poker chips, girl. If he's out there, they'll put him away for the duration of the war. It's also gonna go hard on Micah and Ester Cooley. They've been sheltering a Yank. They're good people, but their boy's in the Union Army. That fact won't sit well hereabouts."

"What will happen to Micah and Ester?" I ask.

"India," Doctor Hooks says, "there's a lot of them rogue men here full of hate for everyone. Especially poor Negroes who helped the Yanks and is eatin' bacon and eggs. They'll string 'em up to a tree branch and set a fire under them. I swear they will." He spits into the bushes. "The Spreckles have told the world that Micah and Ester inherited ten acres of Trimble land. That's illegal in the South, for coloreds to own white man's land."

"It's completely legal," I say. "Mr. Pardoe filed the will and the papers himself, and Julia told me herself! My pa witnessed it with his signature."

Doctor Hooks just smiles as if he hadn't heard. "They had better find your Yank here, India. He's an officer. He can be exchanged for two of ours."

In the moonlight I follow Junius Hooks out to Micah and Ester's cabin. He rattles the door until Micah lets him in.

I hear almost nothing when the speaking is in the cabin, but Doctor Hooks's parting shot flies over the landscape. He strides out of the cabin yelling.

"You got no deed to your ten acres, Micah Cooley. Every

miserable scrap you own, including the shirt on your back, will be confiscated if you don't hand over that Yank by morning. You and Ester think on it now. It's not my fault and it's not my doing, but you know what the local boys do to coloreds when they get wind of them helping the enemy."

"I've heard tell," I hear Micah say drily.

Doctor Hooks pleads with Ester. "And they'll catch him anyway. He's a cripple. He can't go three hundred yards by hisself! Save your life, woman. Use your head!"

When I find Henry, he is crying in my hammock. "I have done nothing but make trouble. Trouble for people who saved my life." Henry swears in words I didn't reckon would ever come out of a church choirmaster. "The Home Guard'll do something terrible to Micah and Ester."

"No, sir," I say. "They won't have a chance. We will take you up the Pike and over into Harpers Ferry tonight. Ester and Micah have got a mule and a wagon. No one will stop an old Negro couple with hay in their cart. "

Henry lets this go through his mind. "They've been done out of even this little bit of burned-up land they're trying to bring back to life," he says.

There is a full moon. The grandfather clock in the corner of the front room has been spared by the Yanks and continues to tick away the minutes, as if they were full of the shouts and songs of its family.

There is no time for talk or the collecting of small possessions. There is only time to get Henry into the wagon and to hitch Maybelle and leave.

Micah drives entirely too slowly for my taste, but we cannot risk disturbing Henry's newly healed leg. Ester walks beside us to lighten the load on the wagon. We don't go any speedier than her sauntering walk. We are still inside Confederate territory near western Virginia when Henry's leg begins to bleed. We stop to give him a change of dressing. Micah bends over him. Then quite suddenly we smell tobacco smoke in the road.

There are two men with fast horses. They raise a cloud of dust and stand within it. I can see only their outlines, blurred against the moonlit field beside us, but the lighted tip of a cigar glows in the blackness.

"Home Guard! Halt right where you are!" says the taller of the figures. "Y'all have a fugitive Yank here?"

The other man tries to light a cigarette and misses. In the flame's range I see them swaying comfortably in their cavalry saddles. Their horses are fat and happy, probably stolen from a Yankee supply train. We are ordered to put our hands in the air.

We do not answer but let the night wind sing.

Finally Henry says, "I give myself up. Do not arrest or hurt these people."

"We gonna do just whatever it is we wanna do," says the littler man. "Cute little girl, n_____ man, Yankee officer. I can tell you what order we gonna do it in!" His voice is glee-ful. "We got guns on you so don't move."

"My friend is badly wounded," I yell shrilly at them. "If you are going to take him then take him carefully."

"Hey, little cutie!" says guard one. "You're mine first!"

For a moment another match flares in front of his face. I can see him grin, rat's teeth shining, face all freckled and porky.

Unseen, Ester stands in the hay field twenty yards away. Ester has Henry's service revolver. She reaches into her skirt. The shots jolt across the countryside in the pristine night.

Ester draws a cross in the dust where the men lie. She kneels and asks God to forgive them and to forgive her. Her back is straight as a rod as she prays. Holding Henry, I am certain of one thing. This killing will not rest in any secret room in Ester's memory. It will likely be a story polished and repeated to her grandchildren and from them to great-grandchildren.

We hitch the militia horses to the back of our wagon. Micah tries to make Henry comfortable, leaning him against the men's saddle blankets. He uncorks the thick brown bottle of laudanum and gives him a last swallow. We go creaking on our way.

Ester is the first to speak. It is after we cross into Yankee territory. "Two good riding horses! And two good cavalry saddles," says Ester. "Micah and me, we'll keep 'em, if you don't mind."

They leave us at the entrance of the army post. Micah lifts Henry out of the wagon into the arms of two Yankee picket guards. Then he and Ester melt away, just on the corner of Potomac Street. They flow into a river of sutlers and rovers, freed slaves and orphaned families, all refugees moving steadily, spilling out into western Virginia from the starving South.

"Wait!" I shout, but they do not wait.

Henry stills my calling them with his fingertips on my sleeve. "It is my opinion," says Henry, "that being slaves, Ester and Micah were born with broken hearts. They are looking for their son and for a place to mend those hearts."

My hair is filthy. Henry's wife, Agatha, washes it, cuts it, and dresses it. My tooth is loose in the back, and the army dentist fixes it. My old stained Trimble boy clothes are taken from me, and I am given new dresses. There is to be a story in *Harper's Weekly* about "The Rebel Lass Who Saved a Yank." Henry's wife polishes my nails. "You must look right spiffy for your picture, girl," says Agatha, brushing my hair. "The reporter wants the whole kit and caboodle story from you and Henry, with pictures to go with it."

The bristles tangle in my unkempt hair. Agatha keeps at

it. Her dress has a clean crispness to it that has gone out of Southern clothing years ago. "It is a likely thing," Agatha goes on, "that next Friday in the White House Mr. Lincoln himself will read this very story, India. *Harper's Weekly* is the favorite reading of our dear president."

"I will never be able to return home again if this story gets out," I plead.

"Much worse than this will have to be forgiven after the war," says Agatha, her mouth full of hairpins.

I do not tell Agatha Bedell what we in the South think of President Lincoln, or some of the names we have for him. And to the *Harper's Weekly* man I just describe Ester and Micah Cooley, whose work it was to bring Henry safely north. But the *Harper's Weekly* man doesn't want to hear about Ester and Micah. He wants the Rebel lass's story, and it matters not a word what I say because he has composed most of it ahead of time anyway.

Agatha and Henry ask me to come to Vermont with them and wait out the war. "No," I say. "I must visit my pa's grave and mark it. Then I'll be off to Ohio." I kiss them good-bye and promise to visit someday. Will I ever see them again? Will I ever see my mother again?

In my tent the light is strained to yellow through the white canvas. My eight-foot-by-five-foot space is kitted out with a small turkey carpet, a cot, and a locker. I have brought Maybelle to the army farrier for shoes. She needs some purple gentian for a sore on her back. I must red her up to take me five hundred miles to Ohio.

I am awaked by a twitching of the tent flap and a distinctly Virginia voice that says "Hello?" and coughs politely.

I didn't ever expect to see him again. When I look into his eyes I am unable to speak. He takes off his cap and asks, "Remember me?"

"What do you want of me?" I answer, faltering.

"*Harper's Weekly* has hired me to draw your portrait," says Captain Strother. "They want a portrait to accompany their story. You are quite the little heroine, Miss Moody. All the powers that be read *Harper's Weekly* and they will hear of your adventures."

"Hell will freeze over before I pose for you, Captain Strother!" I snap.

Strother smiles. "Now that is just the expression I want you to keep on your face, please, Miss Moody," says Strother. "Just that flashing anger is perfect!"

"I won't do it!" I repeat.

"I can help you, Miss Moody."

"How could you possibly help me even if I wanted you to?" I ask, ready to spit in his eye.

"I know where Emory Trimble is," says Strother.

PORTE CRAYON

Captain Strother guides me into the parade ground, where he has already set up a velvet upholstered chair and a Greek column for my elbow.

"Emory Trimble was killed at Wilderness!" I answer.

"Not true," says Strother. "Emory is very much alive, Miss Moody. Now, will you sit for me?"

I cannot breathe evenly and Strother has to tell me to stop smiling because he wants an anxious look on my face.

He busies himself setting up his easel. His fingers spin the wing nuts and flanges deftly. Then the whole awkward pile of wooden easel legs straighten up into a support for his drawing pad. On the back of his portfolio case, written in fancy script is, *Porte Crayon*, which I have to guess is his pen name. "Emory Trimble is working as a medic in Point Lookout Prison. It's in Maryland out on the peninsula," Strother says casually.

"How far is that?"

"Not far from Baltimore. As it happens I must go

immediately to Baltimore to the printer when this portrait is finished. If you behave yourself, Miss Moody, and sit still for this portrait, I will personally escort you there."

"How long will this take?" I ask him. The chair is lumpy and damp and I don't want to sit in it. He moves me to a piece of artillery, a Napoleon gun on wheels that has been abandoned in the middle of the camp. "This is a more dramatic setting anyway," he says. "Now then, 'The Rebel maid who risks all to save the noble Vermont lieutenant from certain death behind enemy lines.' Try to keep that in mind."

"It was all Ester and Micah Cooley who did the hard part," I answer. "Weren't me so much, David Strother. I told the interview man that. I hope he writes about them, too."

Strother begins to make large strokes in charcoal.

"Can I get up and see what you are doing?" I ask.

"Not until it's finished. About an hour," he tells me. "Point Lookout is a very dangerous place. No woman would be allowed within ten miles of it."

Strother keeps drawing, eyes first on me then on the paper, switching back and forth, his hand busy and fast. At last he cleans his fingers of the charcoal on a rag and lights a small cigar.

"I turned my back when Geneva Trimble was about to be shipped off to Louisville Prison," he says in a voice that seems to seek my approval. "She is in Winchester with Calvin until the war is over."

"When will that ever be?" I ask.

Strother cocks his head and rubs out some of his lines. "The war is really over now, Miss Moody. General Sherman has about destroyed Georgia and is starting on the Carolinas. General Longstreet, General Hood, and Nathan Bedford Forrest are nearly finished. They have no armies. General Lee alone is left. He cannot stand against Grant for more than three months. So I would say by spring. Then we can expect a welcome stillness in the land for a thousand miles around."

"I will go to wherever Point Lookout might be," I say. "I will find a map and take my horse, Maybelle, and ride there if it takes ten days."

Strother simply says, "Have a glass of water. It makes the mouth easier to draw. Sit back please, Miss Moody."

"But . . ."

Strother ignores me. He says, "Point Lookout Prison allows no visitors. You would never be allowed to see Emory or even get him a message. The provost of Point Lookout is Colonel John Patterson. Patterson's a friend," says Strother. "I'll get you in."

I want so badly to say no to Strother. But I say yes.

The portrait is soon done. As he packs it carefully away under glassine paper, Strother says, "I warn you, Point Lookout is the most terrible of prisons. What is there should not be seen by a young lady like you."

"I was at Sharpsburg," I growl back at him. "I was looking for my pa the night of the battle. There is nothing in the world I haven't seen, Captain Strother."

He wipes his hand across his mouth, folds his easel up, and nods with a little respect that I think is not pretended.

David Strother has U.S. Army railway passes.

"I can pay my own way, thank you," I tell him.

Strother is amused. "How much money do you have?" he asks.

I say, "One dollar and fifty cents."

"Confederate dollars?"

"Yes."

He laughs. I nearly hit him.

The train starts up and pulls out of the Harpers Ferry Station. I have never been on a railway train in my life. The cars go much faster and smoother than even a four-horse phaeton. "How much does it cost to go by train to Ohio?" I ask.

Strother shows me to a seat and sits next to me, one leg in the aisle. "To Ohio?" he asks.

"I intend to go to Oberlin College, where they admit women into their degree program. I'll ride my horse up to Ohio if I can't afford the train."

Strother whistles. "My dear Miss Moody, if it is not rude of me to say, it would take you most of the winter to get there, and the roads are very unsafe. You would never make it. And if it is not too rude of me to ask, how are you going to be able to pay the fees? You are an orphan from a devastated town. You are homeless and destitute. College would cost a year of your father's salary, and he is dead! Your only recourse, I suppose, is to ask young Mr. Trimble to foot the bill."

"You make me *very* angry, Captain Strother," I answer.

He smiles at me and says, "Anger makes a woman crackle and come alive!"

I turn to him. "Thanks to you, Captain Strother, all the Trimbles' precious things, not to mention Ester and Micah's deed to ten acres, are gone. Because of you, Captain Strother, the entire Trimble estate is ruined and they are penniless. I would never ask Emory for a dime."

The locomotive engine pours out intense black smoke, but the rails beneath us are not torn up by the army and we travel like an arrow to the east and to Baltimore. We pass Frederick, Relay, Ellicot Corners.

The silence between us fairly rings. I wait for another lecture, but it does not come.

"I did a terrible thing that day," admits Strother suddenly.

"Yes, you did."

"I had not intended to do it. My anger got away from me. I regret it."

"It's a mite late to be sorry now," I answer.

"One of the three men that Patrick Reilly executed was my best friend. I could not help my anger. Geneva

Trimble is a romantic fool for the Southern cause."

"It didn't bring your friend back to burn all the Trimbles' most precious belongings and break their hearts," I answer.

"No, it did not," he agrees quite humbly. "I know most of the people in the valley will never forgive what I did to Geneva and Calvin Trimble."

"Never," I say.

"But Geneva lied. And the boy she took in was a born killer. He could not be allowed to kill again. Patrick Reilly had blood on his hands."

"His hands were burned to a crisp," I reply.

"War takes all humanity from a man," says Strother with sincerity.

I answer smartly, "Some men!"

He winces. Then David Strother reaches into his trousers pocket. He holds out an army railway pass. "You can have it," he says. "It'll take you anywhere you want to go, free, on the Baltimore and Ohio line."

"Keep your pass," I say, not looking at it.

He twists in his seat, blows a lungful of air out of his cheeks, and says, "You have no doubt been as overtrained in the Scriptures as I have."

I don't answer. I only rock back and forth to the rhythm of the train.

"I'm sure you know the seven deadly sins," Captain Strother says.

"Gluttony, sloth, envy, lust, wrath, greed . . . pride," I answer, hearing my mother's voice.

"Indeed," he says. "My own personal sin is wrath." He takes my hand, opens the fingers forcibly, and places the pass on my palm. "I suspect that your sin is pride." Then he recloses the fingers over the pass.

HELL FROZEN OVER

Emory and I sit on a wooden bench in the small stone anteroom allowed to the officers and medics of Point Lookout prison. The room is freezing cold despite a little fire in the grate. We must be modest in our greeting because there are wardens and other medics who come and go, trying to warm their hands. We sit still, but there is no modesty in Emory's eyes or mine.

"If hell were to freeze over," says Emory, "it would be like this place. India, you must not stay here for a minute more. It is full of disease. Twenty men die in a day in this tomb."

"But you are alive!" I say with such joy.

"I am doing what I can," he says.

I tell him all but the house and piano at Longmarsh are destroyed. Every tree in the orchards. Every scrap of his father's papers. But that his mother and father are safe somewhere in Winchester.

Emory swallows hard. He cannot find words. He smiles with the side of his mouth and asks, "Father did not have heart failure in all this? Mother did not have a stroke?"

"I would say their hearts are broken," I answer. "When they find you alive, Emory, they will mend."

An officer pads into the small room and rubs chapped hands by the fire. He looks at us curiously. "Not many women in this place," he comments curtly.

"It is my sister, sir. I beg to have a moment of privacy," says Emory.

I feel then it will go unremarked if I rest my head against Emory's shoulder.

"All of your notes from the hospital were destroyed," I say.

"I thought so. David Strother appears to have had one of his temper tantrums at Trimble expense," Emory says dryly.

"I am going to Ohio on the train," I say. "Strother gave me an army pass. He seems to feel some remorse at what he did. I took it."

"That money you found on the battlefield should see you through your first year," says Emory.

"I gave it to Mama," I tell him.

Emory makes a *pfft* sound. His arm surrounds my shoulders. "How will you pay your fees?" he asks.

"I will work on the Oberlin College farm."

"It will take you twice as long to get through," he says. "Take this."

Emory twists the gold ring with the double ruby off his finger. "Sell this," he says. "Sell it and use the money to pay the tuition fees. I will come as soon as I can."

"I could never sell it."

"It's wartime, India. There is no room for pride or romantic notions. Sell it when you get to Ohio. Go to a reputable jeweler and get a good price for it, India."

Echoing down the hallway come the cries of one man after another. "Doctor! Doctor, hurry!"

"When will you come?" I ask. "When will they free you from this place, Emory?"

"Oh, I am perfectly free," says Emory. "I am here of my own choice. I am free to go with you, India, and free to tend to my parents and land, which I have to do first. But also," he says, "I am free to stay here and tend these men until the war ends."

Emory Trimble touches my face and brushes his mouth on the parting in my hair, quickly, while the officer is still turned to the fire. Then he guides us both to the doorway. "It will not be long, India," he whispers. "Maybe summer."

A corporal bends around the doorway. Strother has sent him to take me back to the station and the Ohio train.

Emory walks down a stone tunnel with vaulted brick ceilings, mold and moss dripping on its unspeakable walls. He pulls a stethoscope out of his pocket and goes into the room where the man is crying out.

AUTHOR'S NOTE

Red Moon at Sharpsburg is about a real war and real lives. I spent twelve years researching and writing it; there are so many experts on the Civil War that I dreaded getting a detail wrong. I read books and diaries and other first-person accounts of the war in northern Virginia. I visited museums and historical societies devoted to the war, walked the battlefields, attended reenactments, combed through old photographs. Gradually the world in which my story takes place began to come to life for me.

In 1860, time crawled slowly, by our jet-age standards. Mornings, afternoons, and evenings would seem to us empty of stimulation except from nature itself. Slow, hard work and waiting for things to happen filled the hours. Very few people in America owned watches or looked at clocks. Most Americans lived their whole lives never going more than five miles from the house in which they were born. To us, everyone and everything back then would smell terrible because of primitive sanitation.

On the other hand, the English language was beautifully written and elegantly spoken—compared to now—by the educated folk. Virginia farmers and tradespeople spoke terrific country slang. But if I were to write as the people in this book would have actually spoken, nobody would be able to read a word. Most of their real country talk has been lost to time. So I have put their words in language we can understand.

Good, true information was often just not available. Even the doctors, lawyers, and business professionals believed in a mix of old wives' tales about race, gender, superstitions, medicine, science, and everything else around them. The First Lady of the United States, Mary Todd Lincoln, tried to contact her dead son Willie through table-rapping mediums—right in the White House.

The worst of the stupidity and cruelty of the age was slavery itself. The slave owners in the South created a myth of inferiority of the black man that nearly every person at the time took for granted as true. People kept against their will in hunger, fear, filth, and ignorance are not able to appear the equal of their masters.

As my story began to emerge, the characters took over, as characters always do. All the events in this book are based on true events. Henry Bedell really was a Yankee soldier saved by a young Southern woman. Events such as the burning of the Trimbles' possessions really took place. The destruction of the Shenendoah Valley, the medieval state of medicine, the limited opportunities for women, the injustice of slavery—all of that is true.

But I hope that my story will reveal something deeper than fact, and that is the profound immorality of war. We, too, live in a time of war. What happened in Virginia a hundred and fifty years ago is just as relevant as today's television headline news. It is easy to start wars, but much harder to stop them. Sometimes we must fight wars, but it is unforgivable to pump war full of glamour and glory. There are heroes in wartime, but often the true heroes are not soldiers but ordinary people on whose five acres of cornfield the battle happens.

It was my purpose to write about Virginia at war in the 1860s without prettifying it, mindful that our history is, to paraphrase Barbara Tuchman, a lantern shining on the stern of our ship to show us where we have been.

Rosemary Wells
October 2006

BIBLIOGRAPHIC NOTE

An enormous amount has been written about the American Civil War. I read a great deal in order to familiarize myself with the war and with the people of the Shenandoah Valley; much of it was scholarly, obscure, or hard to find. However, the following books were particularly helpful and are more generally accessible.

Personal stories, diaries, and letters from people who lived through the time helped bring the historical period to life for me. Here are some I enjoyed: *Sarah Morgan: The Civil War Diary of a Southern Woman*, edited by Charles East, gives the point of view of an intelligent and well-off Southern belle whose opinions were in many ways typical of her time and place. *A Woman Doctor's Civil War: Esther Hill Hawks' Diary*, edited by Gerald Schwartz, is the authentic diary of a pioneering female doctor, abolitionist, and advocate of women's rights, who risked her life to serve freedmen and black troops of the Union army in the occupied South. *Shenandoah 1862*, one of Time-Life Books Voices of the Civil War series, tells the story of the 1862 Shenandoah campaign through actual soldiers' accounts. *Tara Revisited: Women, War, and the Plantation Legend* by Catherine Clinton draws on letters, diaries, slave narratives, and Southern literature to give a fully rounded picture of antebellum Southern women. *Trials and Triumphs: The Women of the American Civil War* by Marilyn Mayer Culpepper examines the Civil War diaries and letters of more than five hundred women.

Of the many historical studies I consulted, here are some that were very helpful in providing information on military and medical conditions, and on what life was like for women. Bruce Catton's classic Army of the Potomac trilogy—*Mr. Lincoln's Army, Glory Road,* and *A Stillness at Appomattox*—covers the military history of the Civil War in balanced and fascinating detail. *A Pictorial Encyclopedia of Civil War Medical Instruments and Equipment* by Gordon Dammann shows what would have been available to doctors of the time. Christie Anne Farnham's *The Education of the Southern Belle: Higher Education and Student Socialization in the Antebellum South* looks at the opportunities available for Southern girls and how educational expectations were different from those in the North. And Jean H. Baker's *Mary Todd Lincoln: A Biography* gives a sympathetic portrait of the president's wife, including her interest in Spiritualism.

Fictional accounts give another view of the era. *Civil War Women: The Civil War Seen Through Women's Eyes,* edited by Frank McSherry, Jr., is a collection of short stories by women, including some like Louisa May Alcott who were there at the time. *The Dreams of Mairhe Mehan* and *Mary Mehan Awake* by Jennifer Armstrong, follow the story of a fictional Irish immigrant girl struggling to survive in Washington, D.C., during the war and immediately after. And *Enemy Women*, by Paulette Jiles, is a novel about an eighteen-year-old from Missouri falsely imprisoned as a Confederate spy.

My thanks to the authors of all of these books.